Matters of the Heart-Autumn

Lucy Heath

MATTERS OF THE HEART

SEASONS OF LOVE

Lucy Heath

BOOK 2: AUTUMN

The façaded Heart

Dedication

To everyone who is going through a season of rejection, or abandonment, if God hasn't moved you—stand still…

L. Heath

Lucy Heath

All Scripture quotations, unless otherwise indicated, are taken from the Holy Bible, King James Version [KJV] public domain.

DISCLAIMER

Names and personalities mentioned in this novel come solely from characters developed from the author's creativity. They are purely fictional, and in no way depict the lives, situations, and living areas of known or unknown persons.

Introduction

I wish I could say that life is not like the scripture text in Ecclesiastes chapter three. Fortunately, or unfortunately depending on how you view your personal situations, the Word is true. Life does have its seasons, and I believe that includes your love life as well. Some of us get through this season better than others. Some come out victors. Some get stuck. And others— well, they suffer heart break after heart break.

Love feels great when you are on the sunny side of the street– when everything's going well, and you're on top of your game. But there are some for whom that didn't happen— at least not yet, and they are the ones who may be muddling through their season with an anguishing heart. It may be easy to tell them to just get over it! It's so easy to say, but they must first understand that the ultimate Love–is **Agape**. Medical technology along with the help of clinical psychologist lets us know that heart break can feel very real, and may display itself in real physical emotions.

The Medical terminology for 'broken heart syndrome' is **Takotsubo Cardiomyopathy**, *or another name is* 'Stress Cardiomyopathy'.

According to the Mayo Clinic—one may have sudden chest pains, or think they are having a heart attack because of a traumatic experience that can alter the heart rate, and–or causing it to become irregular. While it is not directly related to one of the seasons in this novel where the character goes through sorrowful disappointments in her love life; one can determine that the agony of heart break is real, and can lead to mental, or physical issues if sustained, or goes unattended.

Reviewing Ecclesiastes, and know that there is a time to keep, and a time to cast away. Those who live a happy, healthy life are those who admit that there are some things they can't get through alone. But what if you're like the 'autumn'—the cool chilling air that causes the *beautiful falling leaves to crackle under your feet, and each crunch reminds you of one failed relationship after another.*

So it is with our characters who want to know if they will ever come to know again the solace of love that now seemed to wane from them. Yes, waning even in the love they once had for the Lord. Is this a passing season, or do they just settle in and accept their fates of happenstance?

To that question the Lord answered—

To everything there is a season, and a time to every purpose under the heaven:

A time to be born, and a time to die; a time to plant, and a time to pluck up that which is planted;

A time to kill, and a time to heal; a time to break down, and a time to build up;

A time to weep, and a time to laugh; a time to mourn, and a time to dance;

A time to cast away stones, and a time to

gather stones together; a time to embrace, and a time to refrain from embracing;

A time to get, and a time to lose; a time to keep, and a time to cast away;

A time to rend, and a time to sew; a time to keep silence, and a time to speak;

A time to love, and a time to hate; a time of war, and a time of peace.

He hath made everything beautiful in his time: He hath set the eternity in the heart of men...

I know that, whatsoever God doeth, it shall be forever: nothing can be put to it; nor anything taken from it: and God doeth it, that men should fear before him.

Ecclesiastes 3:1-8, 11a, 14 [kjv]

Prologue

The condition of the heart is a major concern of God. Before we begin with our story, I would like to introduction a few scriptures from the King James Version of the Bible for your consideration.

Proverbs 3:5

Trust in the LORD will all your heart and lean not to your own understanding.

Proverbs 4:23

Above all else, guard your heart, for out of it flows the issues of life.

Psalm 51:10

Create in me a pure heart, O God, and renew a steadfast spirit within me.

Psalm 73:26

My flesh and my heart may fail, but God is the strength of my heart and my portion forever.

Proverbs 23:26

My son, give me your heart and let your eyes delight in my ways.

Psalm 19:14

May the words of my mouth and the

meditation of my heart be acceptable in your sight, O LORD, my strength and my redeemer.

How many times have we read these scriptures and not considered how much God really cares about the condition of our heart. He wants our hearts to be whole and healthy spiritually, as well as physically.

I love that the heart is protected within the chest cavity, because if it were not, it would be exposed to the elements of nature just like the human flesh. I dare say it would not survive through the first stages of its infancy. It should give us great pleasure to know that we not only have the physical frame to protect our heart, but we also have the Word of God.

Medical journals report that the normal heart rate for adults can range from 60 to 100 beats per minute. But with the lovelorn heart, the broken heart—each and every beat brings back the hurtful pang of what could have been if love had stayed. When our heart aches because of love lost; we sometimes forget that *Agape* Love is still there.

If it weren't so odd, it would be downright ironic the way people's lives are like the seasons. I know most of us think about the four major seasons of the year: *spring, summer, fall (autumn)*, and *winter;* but somehow I personally believe there are more than just those four. There are the seasons of transitioning that come during the in-between times. Those seasons of change are the ones we don't hear much about—however they do exist. Maybe we can feel them more than we can pinpoint them, or give them a name. That time for Casandra is the façade of *autumn*.

Autumn is not like other seasons. It can fool you into false hope—at least that's the way it was for her. Autumn looks bright and warming. *Her* colors are brilliantly displayed in an array of vividly changing leaves. The leaf, once a lively green, now begins to gradually change. Almost unnoticed at first, a lone leaf may begin to morph at its base to sport its burnt orange hue, and another–its golden yellow alterations. Yes, the fall of the year can come in very gently, but once it hits her peak, there's nothing elusive about it. You know *it* has arrived!

Autumn is beautiful with her coat of many colors. It's full of life, hope and sunshine. But that's only her deception. Because right when the leaves look full of vim and vigor-they fall from their limbs to a certain death. Then on the ground their brightness fades, and they begin to turn brown. There is nothing left to look forward to but the loneliness of their demise. Its brilliant color is no longer recaptured as it is trampled and crushed under foot, or blow away by the wind. *"Oh, how I wish the bright leaves would stay"*

Chapter 1

Casandra sat at the luncheon sized table in her small kitchen. She nibbles on the cookies she'd wrapped in the napkin and stuck in her purse. She and a couple of her coworkers had gone to the buffet style restaurant for their one hour lunch break. Not only had she gone back for seconds, but got extra cookies to take home for a late night snack. She really didn't need that second go round from the buffet, nor the extra cookie snack, because she had already eaten two cookies.

Casandra decided to save the six more cookies for her daughter's after school snack. Usually on her way home from work she would pick Darla up from the after-school program, but on Tuesdays and Thursdays Darla also stayed for the free tutoring program. She was an okay student, but this year her school work became a little more challenging for her. She would be going to Middle school next year, and Casandra wanted her grades to be up to par in math and English.

Not living far from the school on tutoring days she always went home for the hour and a half wait.

Her apartment loaned itself to a pretty nice view. was on the front of the building, so she had a nice large window from the side view of the living room, and also a large window in the kitchen. When she sat in the kitchen she could see most of the main street; the publi bus stop, and the small park across the street. The date on the calendar were nearing the middle of September, and although the days were not blazing hot, the month still had some warm days to enjoy. It was the nights tha had begun to cool some.

'Pretty soon it will be autumn'. She had no idea what made her think of the 'outdated' word. Now-a-days people just say *fall.* Casandra felt a slight smile curl around her mouth–remembering that that was the word her grandmother used to use. *Autumn.* When she was a little girl autumn was her favorite time of year. That was before she really understood what the end results meant, and attached the season to all the hurts and discouragements that filtered into her life as an adult. Now most of her life felt like autumn—the season between summer and winter. Webster's dictionary defines it as a season (a time) of maturity and incipient decline. *'Well, he sure hit that nail on the*

head! Nothing feels more true to me than the last part of that definition.'

At twenty-eight years old she felt like an old, unattractive divorcee. This was one of the days she felt that anything that might have had a chance of 'budding' in her life was on a sluggish decline. Casandra reached for another donut. Stopping by the donut store on the way home, she convinced herself to get something sweet for herself since she was saving the cookies for her daughter. She promised herself she would eat no more than two of them today, and save the rest for tomorrow— however the half dozen was already half gone. *Why do I do this to myself?*

The more she thought about the way her life was turning out, the angrier she became. She sat for a few moments reflecting on the short happy moments she experienced when Raymond showed some interest in her. But when that faded so did her hope for happiness. The constant rejection was a relentless reminder of how much she loathed men. *They are all dogs*—"Yes", she said aloud, "Dogs."

Many a time Casandra aligned her life with the season of autumn. On the outside she carried the colorful, cheerful façade of the changing leaves;

while on the inside she felt the dreadful resolve of spending another autumn alone and depressed waiting for the cold, damp winter to set in—only to bury herself like a hibernating bear.

———

The familiar ringtone of her cellphone sounded, and Casandra reached for her purse. Her usual nature of the over-protective mother kicked in assuming it was the school calling with news of something negative happening to Darla. She couldn't explain why she felt that way, because nothing like that had ever happened. She nervously picked up the phone, and viewed the caller ID. She slid the arrow upward to receive the call. It was from Lucinda, her friend from church. Casandra didn't have many of what one might call *close* friends, but Lucinda was the next best thing to it. It wasn't that people didn't try to be friendly toward her, it's just that she wasn't, or didn't care to be a very sociable person.

Lucinda was a couple of years her senior, and such a great encourager. A person couldn't help but to be drawn to her. She was calling to remind her of the *'Singles'* meeting that was to be held on this coming Wednesday evening. Instead of attending the regular scheduled Bible study, the 'Singles, or Single Again 'populous could once a month on Wednesdays attend the *Singles* meeting.

Restoration of Hope Christian Ministry tried several times to develop a ministry for the single population of their congregation—however for some reason or another it just didn't fly. It was when Deacon Campbell and his wife Belinda stepped in to head up the 'Singles' ministry that the ministry began to take on more interest.

The Campbell's had a heart and a passion to work with the young adult ministry. Deacon Anthony said he and his wife prayed about extending their services in the church, and were surprised when the Lord laid on their hearts the *Singles* Ministry. They knew it was very unusual—if not unheard of for a married couple to head up this type of ministry in the church, but they knew to trust God and His promptings.

Casandra thanked Lucinda for the call, and told her she would think about attending the upcoming meeting. She remembered it was

Lucinda who coerced her to go along with her to the meeting last month. She really wasn't interested in becoming socially active in the church, or in any other place for that matter. She didn't do *face book*, *Instagram, snap chat, twitter, skype, facetime,* or post anything on any of the other social outlets. She had her cell phone, and an email address in case the school wanted to get in touch with her. Casandra felt she didn't have anybody to reach out to anyway, and she didn't want anybody trying to reach out to her!

She attended Bible study (most of the time) and Sunday morning services. She decided that was good enough for her and Darla—at least for the time being. At the last 'Singles' meeting she attended they wanted her to put her email address and phone number down on the sign-in sheet so she could be included in the E-blast and group text messages, but she wasn't ready for that either. As a matter of fact—she wasn't sure if she was even going to attend any more meetings. She only went the first time so Lucinda would stop asking her about it.

Chapter 2

Realizing the time, Casandra pushed back from the table and reached for her purse. Haskell Elementary School was only a ten minute drive away from the apartment, but she still had to get a move on. She reached the school and parked across the street from the main entrance. She went down the corridor where the fifth grade hallway was located, and on to Mr. Williams' classroom. He taught after-school tutoring for fourth and fifth graders. When she got to the room, Darla was packed and ready to go. Casandra signed the sheet on the clipboard with her name and the time she signed Darla out. She thanked Mr. Williams for his devotion and time, and then left the building.

On the way home she wished she had used that extra hour she had to prepare something for dinner. That was her original intention, but she began to eat the donuts, two of Darla's cookies and then the phone call came in. After that—well, she just sat there musing over negative feelings, and feeling depressed. The sweets had killed her hunger for the moment; however she knew her daughter would be wanting something to snack on. Remembering the wrapped up cookies in her purse, she took a couple of them out of the napkin, and gave them to Darla. She would wait until after dinner to give her the remaining few.

Casandra drove into her assigned parking space on the north side of the building and parked her car. She was pondering over what to fix for dinner. When she unlocked the door to her apartment, she went straight to the kitchen, and sent Darla to her room to finish any other homework she still had to do.

———

Lucinda wanted to say more to Casandra, but she decided to wait until another time. She understood that between work, taking care of her daughter, and other obligations—it was hard for Casandra to get some personal *'me'* time in on the side.

Casandra and her siblings were partially raised by their grandparents. The grandparents still lived in the state—however her grandfather was suffering with several illnesses which called for her grandmother to step in as his primary care-giver. Because of that, Casandra felt it would be too much of a burden on them to babysit Darla if she wanted to go somewhere. So instead–she just stayed home, or took Darla with her whenever she went somewhere. Lucinda wanted to treat her friend to lunch, or an evening out to dinner and a movie. She thought that would be a way for her to relax and have some *'girl talk'*. She just had to pray about a good time to do it.

Lucinda had a sense of what Casandra was going through. She didn't want to come off as being a busy-body, but she did want to be a good friend. She thought about some of the character signs of being overwhelmed, or even of slight depression she saw Casandra going through. These were symptoms that she was once challenged with, and had now overcome. Although she wasn't a single parent, she too had come through a few bad relationships. Lucinda was nearly devastated by her last relationship, and found herself on a downward spiral of low self-esteem. That's when she was rescued by a *now* good friend at the church who demonstrated to her genuine *agape* love, and the nurturing help that came through the Word of God.

She was grateful for Pastor Hastings and Restoration of Hope Christian Ministry. The members were loving and seemed genuinely concerned for her as a person. The 'Singles' ministry was revived about six months ago. Lucinda had been a member there for almost four years now—long enough to see one of the previous efforts for a 'Singles' ministry flop. That might be why she declined Belinda's first efforts to get her to join in with the *Singles*. She thought to herself, *'who needs to sit around with a group of single women, because the guys who were single, and just as miserable as the ladies rarely attended those sort of meetings.* Of course that's not how it came off with Deacon Anthony and Belinda Campbell. Even though they were a married couple, they didn't make it seem like being single was a communal sin.

The meetings were not some sort of *dating game* strategy either. Each of them could share about their individual takes on singleness. During the fellowship they came to discover that there were different *types,* or causes for people being single. Some of those people were very secure in their singleness; while others were not.

The Campbell's (who also had a degree in counseling) were geared toward building a sense of self-worth and confidence in the group so they could feel that they were vital to the church body, and an intricate part of the kingdom of God. Lucinda tried to remember if it was at the second, or third meeting when the Campbell's gave a homework assignment to the group. The assignment was to learn more about people in the Bible who were single. That surly was one of the different things about their Single's meetings. Lucinda remembers being surprised to find so many single men and women in the Bible who were used by God; especially since being a barren woman, or an unmarried male–having no offspring carried a much different stigma in biblical times than it did today.

They chose people from an abbreviated list of biblical names selected by the instructors, and were told that during their next meeting the group would play a guessing game. They were to be creative in reporting on their character while the others had to guess, **Who Am I?**

The Campbell's' enjoyed it so much they decided to ask the pastor if the *Singles* could present an expanded dramatization of what they had done in the way of a Sunday afternoon program. Pastor Henrietta loved the idea, and thought it not only would stir interest in the

'Singles' Ministry, but also serve as an evangelistic outreach effort for the church.

———

After dinner Casandra checked Darla's homework and tested her on her spelling words. She made sure Darla had taken her bath, and then allowed her a half hour of computer time before going to bed. Casandra knew that her daughter wanted an iPad, or a lap-top of her own, but right now that wasn't possible. If she could cut back on a few things (not that she was frivolous when it came to money) she could save a little more money hopefully surprising Darla with either one or the other items for Christmas. But for the moment, household expenses and everyday obligations were her top priority.

Casandra lay in bed looking up at the ceiling. She wondered which was the worse of two evils; to have stayed married to her ex-husband while being abused–yet having most of the things she needed (which included having her expenses met), or being divorced and struggling? She decided being divorced and struggling was best—at least she was safe and had peace.

The next day Casandra sat in the breakroom for her fifteen minute break. She usually had some sort of sweet snack sitting in front of her to munch on, but today she didn't. She unwrapped a stick of chewing gum and popped it in her mouth. *Either way,* she thought, none of the things she chose were good for her. *The sweets were bad for her health and caused her to gain weight, and the gum caused some of her filling to weaken and come loose.* She took the gum out and put it in the crinkled foil wrapper laying on the table then got up and threw it in the trash can.

Before she went back to her seat, she went over to the water dispenser. She reached for a paper cup, pushed the 'cold' side lever down and filled the small cup. She checked her cell phone for the time and saw she had almost seven more minutes left before she had to go back to work.

Casandra looked around the breakroom noting that she was the only one there. That was odd because usually there was at least one other people in there when she was just coming in, or when she was about to leave. She went back to where she had been sitting, and took a couple of sips from the paper cup. Thinking again about her health situation, an idea popped into her head. She looked over at the water dispenser and her eyes zeroed in on the 'red' push down lever. "That's it" she said aloud. "I can bring some of those soup cups you add hot water to, and maybe I'll bring some flavored teas." *It may not be the greatest diet plan in the world—but at least it's better than sweets, and it's a start!*

Chapter 3

Antoinette called her sister early on Saturday morning. "Hi Sis. I know it's early, but what time does the Fall Festival at Darla's school start?" Casandra told her sister the festival would start around 9:00am. Her sister and brother-in-law were very supportive when it came to Darla's school activities. Casandra said goodbye to her sister, and rushed to the oven to pull out the cookie sheet. *Good, they didn't get too brown.* The sugar cookies were browned a little around the edges, but they were passable.

Casandra agreed to bake six dozen cookies for the 'Cake Walk'. The donations were to be varieties of desserts and sweets; including cupcakes, brownies, cakes and pies. Darla wanted cupcakes, but Casandra convinced her daughter that cookies would be better. Darla helped to put the orange and multi-color sprinkles on the cookies when they came out of the oven. Then she helped scoop them off the cooling rack so her Mom could put them in the containers.

Casandra lined the round tins with waxed paper, and carefully places each cookie in the tins– putting a sheet of waxed paper between each row. The three large tins held two dozen cookies each.

Knowing that kids always want to buy things at school events, she had already set aside ten dollars in spending money for Darla. The PTA (Parents & Teachers Association) had a well-planned festival with many different venues and activities. There was an area designated for the younger children in kindergarten through second grade—even though they could participate in other events as long as they were supervised by a parent, or an older sibling.

One of the parents attending did children's parties as a sideline, and he was making balloon animals and funny balloon hats for the kids. There was a booth for face painting and a long table was set up where children could string together beads to make jewelry for their mom's. The cost was $2.00.

Another area was set up for the third and fourth graders where they could bounce in the big air balloon house without the guidance of their parents, but still there was an attendant there to watch over them. The fifth and six graders could participate in teams of *Tug-of-war, throwing Darts at ballons,* and what some considered the most fun of all—trying to throw a baseball hard enough at the target to dunk their teachers, or the principal in a tank filled with water.

The weather was still quite warm for it to be the middle of September—maybe because it was the particular part of the year that her grandparents used to call *Indian summer.* Casandra greeted a few of the parents and their children. Some of them she knew from school meetings and activities, but other faces were more familiar because they were also members of her church.

Antoinette and her husband had to leave around twelve o'clock. BJ (their toddler) was tuckered out, and Anthony had another appointment to keep. When all was said and done the Fall Festival at Haskell Elementary school went very well, and a good time was had by all.

———

Now that Darla was bathed and off to bed,

Casandra laid out a few selections for her daughter to choose from to wear to church, and then went to her bedroom to do the same for herself. Having completed that task, she put a disc in the DVD player in the living room. Until recently it would have been a movie about *Romance,* but not tonight. She dragged her exhausted body to the recliner opposite the flat screen TV, and flopped down. For someone who was supposed to be conscious of her weight, she knew taking those few peanut butter cookies to munch on was a big *no no,* but she did it anyway.

Darla won a coconut cake, and a sweet potato pie in the Cake walk; of which Casandra decided to put in the freezer for Thanksgiving. Darla used her money to buy a corn dog, a red candy apple, played the throwing darts game, and brought a secret gift for her mom.

Casandra thought about how she used to be a *true* romantic, but after so many disappointments it was challenging to think of love in a positive way. Through her eyes of hurt and a *façaded* heart, love had not been kind, and it certainly was something she didn't need to dwell on. After all—she thought, *Love isn't for everyone. Everybody doesn't fall in love—whatever that means. Some people just fall into a relationship and think it is love—like stupid 'ol me. Now look at yourself,* she chided. *The relationship ended, and he's gone on his merry way while I had to live every day wounded, dealing with emotional flashbacks.*

Casandra began to feel drowsy. At that point she knew it was time to move from her chair to the bedroom. She said a short prayer before she stood to her feet, and then made her way to the bathroom to brush her teeth before retiring. Laying there with her eyes wide open, her mind kept wandering from one thing to another—*the festival, her job, her daughter, her life… somebody to love.* She resolved to close her eyes and to pray for much needed sleep instead.

The last thing she remembered before sleep set in, was her mind wandering off to a portion of conversation she once had with Antoinette. It had taken place a couple of years after her husband divorced her. Antoinette was saying, '*You remember Mom used to say—"falling in love is easy if you fall in love with the right person."* She than told her sister *that* surly didn't happen to her, so it couldn't be true, and Antoinette said, '*Just because it didn't, or hasn't happen to you, doesn't mean it's not true. Don't give up on love—it'll be true when the right person comes along*'.

Casandra's heavy eyelids began to falter, and

she turned on her side. In that cradled position she knew it wouldn't be long before sleep would come.

———

Sunday morning brought a fresh outlook on life. The first thing on the agenda was to thank the Holy Spirit for keeping her through the night. She greeted *Trinity* with a praise. If nothing else was imbedded in her from her being partly raised by her grandparents—thanking the Lord for His safe keeping was the first course of the day-every day. She knew to do this before her feet hit the floor, and she taught her daughter to do the same.

Sunday breakfast was always scaled down from what they had during the week; not only because they saved their larger meal for when they came home, but an *overly* full stomach could cause drowsy eyes in the middle of church service. She usually had a cup of coffee and a bagel to hold her over, and a selection of boxed breakfast cereal with milk was Darla's choice.

The weather was a bit on the chilly side, but not quite what one could call cold. Casandra moistened her hair with her special moisturizer. She brushed the sides towards the back and she pinned it in a knotted twist. She applied a flattering touch of make up to her face. She never was one to go all-out heavy with her makeup, nor did she try to keep up with the changing trends and the latest fads. From the *'get-go'* her grandmother encouraged her to *'do'* her, and not to be influenced by everyone and everything she saw—especially on TV, and in magazine ads. She checked to see if Darla was dressed and ready for breakfast. Her daughter turned on the television to watch some Sunday morning cartoons. She positioned her chair at the kitchen table so she would be able to watch the animated Bible stories while she ate.

Casandra started the coffee maker, and darted back to her bedroom to finish dressing for church. She selected a black straight wool skirt, a tan and brown sweater set; and added gold tone earrings and a large drop style necklace. She stepped into her black and brown *'Spectator'* heels, slipped on her watch and a gold tone bangle bracelet—then headed back to the kitchen. By that time Darla had rinsed her cereal bowl, placed it in the dishwasher, and moved to the living room to sit in front of the TV.

Casandra hummed one of her favorite gospel tunes as she removed the cream cheese spread from the refrigerator. She pushed the blueberry bagel down in the toaster and poured coffee in her favorite cup. Within a few minutes she was seated at the table with her light breakfast. She said a prayer over her meal, and checking the time she reached for the small bread shaped container in the center of the table. She pulled out one of the cards to read its daily sayings. *"Humm"*, she read aloud, <u>"He who guards his lips, guards his life, but he who speaks rashly will come to ruin"</u> Proverbs 13:3 NIV.

Well, she said to herself—*that's good wisdom, and a point well taken. Thanks grandma!*

Chapter 4

Casandra parked the car and looked at the clock on the dashboard. *Good,* she thought. It was just 10:45am. Church service began at 11:00am. So she had arrived in a reasonable amount of time before the service would start. She took a few minutes to reflect on her grandparent's heeding about not being late to church. Her grandfather used to say: *'Don't come straggling in like God is waiting on you. You should be in your place and waiting to hear from Him.'* She didn't know how true the 'God waiting on you' part was, but it did feel better to be on time, and not interrupting the service by coming in late.

When she came out of her musing, she heard Darla rushing her along—although she hadn't stopped walking toward the building. It was just that her daughter was overly eager to get in the sanctuary to get a good seat near the front. It was youth, and young adult Sunday, and the youth choir was going to be singing. Casandra knew that

Darla wanted to join the choir. She had a beautiful singing voice, but joining the choir meant getting her to rehearsals, and that would place yet another burden on her shoulders. She knew it wasn't fair to her daughter. She brought her to Sunday school, but only on the Sundays when her own class met—the second and forth Sundays. Casandra thought she would attend the next 'Singles' meeting and ask Lucinda, or Sister Belinda if there was anything else happening on that same evening that Darla could be involved in.

The Usher led them to available seating on a pew that was just three rows from the front of the church. Casandra had begun to sit with Lucinda every now and then, but she didn't want to ask her to move just to come sit with her and Darla. People were still coming in for service—some were standing in groups of two or three greeting each other while others were trying to scurry for a seat before the *'Call to Worship'* started.

After they were seated, Darla looked around searching for some of the few kids she went to school with. All of them didn't necessarily live in her neighborhood just because they attended the same school together, however they did go to the same church. Her friend Ellen had a brother in the third grade, and another brother who would be graduating from middle school next year.

Darla's other friend was Princess. She didn't know why her mother gave her that name. To Darla, it sounded more like a title than a name—maybe that's why some of the teachers (the prejudice ones) didn't like to call on her. They didn't want it to seem like they were calling her royalty. Princess was sitting with the youth choir on the front row of chairs in the choir stand. The young adult choir sat on the row behind them.

Pastor Hastings preached a *Harvest* message—"**The Harvest is Plentiful, but the Laborers are Few**", <u>Matthew 9:37</u>. The sermon was to encourage us to get involved in reaching out to others and to become better witnesses for the kingdom of God. We were also to get involved, or better yet—to stay involved in church activities. It seemed that some parishioners' involvement was seasonal; which left a void in fulfilling much needed ministry in the church. Casandra knew the message was speaking to the congregation at large, but being guilty of the matter, she couldn't help but feel the message was directed towards her.

It could have been her imagination, but Casandra thought the church's musician was looking at her. No, it wasn't her imagination, because he looked her way again. She waited a few minutes before turning her eyes away from the pulpit to glance to the area at the left of the stage. When she did, she found Brother Stillwater looking directly at her. He gave her a slight smile, and she quickly turned her head back toward the pulpit area. Brother Marcus played the keyboard, and according to what she often heard, he did it very well.

Now that she thought about it, the one time she attended the 'Singles' meeting, he was there. Her eyes were focused on Pastor Hastings standing behind the podium, but her mind had wandered off in another direction. Her hearing *dulled* because her thoughts were now drawn to the handsome, milk-chocolate complexed man at the keyboard.

Casandra had to snatch her mind back to where it was supposed to be—Church! She scolded herself for jumping to what was most likely a wrong conclusion. She was reminded of the way musicians often look out over the congregation to get a gage on the effectiveness of their music ministry. That was the explanation she came up with. It was reasonably logical—except for one thing. The musicians were not playing at that moment. They were listening to the sermon.

After service Lucinda moved as quickly as she could to try and catch up with Casandra. She wanted to ask her about attending the next 'Singles' meeting. She didn't want to be rude by not acknowledging people who were trying to get her attention, so she slowed her pace and greeted a few of them. When she looked through the scattering congregation, Casandra was nowhere to be seen.

In the car Darla was complaining that she didn't get a chance to speak to any of her friends. Her mother felt really bad about what just happened. She knew her daughter would want to speak with her friends, but after the *Benediction* was pronounced, it looked as if Brother Stillwater was headed in her direction.

She began to panic, and before she knew it she grabbed her purse, Darla's arm, and darted for the first exit she saw. Casandra knew what she did to her daughter wasn't fair. She glanced over at her sitting in the front passenger seat next to her. Darla's arms were folded across her chest, and her bottom lip was poked out in a pout. Casandra didn't know what to say. She couldn't lie and say she had somewhere to go in a hurry—then end up going straight home. She only told her she was sorry for leaving in such a hurry. And then she whispered a prayed to the Lord asking for forgiveness.

Casandra was more peeved with herself than anything else. She knew her fear of emotional involvement was setting up an unhealthy state of mind within herself, but now that she was allowing it to affect her daughter—she knew something had to be done. She needed to talk to someone about it, but who could she trust? The whole thing was puzzling to her. She mainly sat at home in her loneliness wishing she could meet someone nice and caring— yet she was scared to death if it looked like a man wanted to be friendly towards her. '*Yah*', she thought to herself, '*You need help*'.

This was one of those Sunday afternoons when spending a little time at the park seemed like a great idea. Casandra felt badly about rushing away after church service ended—not giving Darla a chance to mingle with her friends. She felt she owed her something in the way of an apology, and staying cooped up inside wouldn't cut it. Besides that, she already felt an eating binge of guilt coming on.

The afternoon was warm and only a slight breeze was stirring. The autumn leaves were striking colors of ruby red, oranges, yellow, and although many still had their waning color of green about them, some of their tip ends were already turning a tannish brown. Casandra suggested they change into their slacks, sneakers, and a comfortable top (accompanied with a cozy sweater), and go for a stroll in the park. Since it was getting past their usual Sunday meal time, Casandra thought a mother-daughter picnic would be nice. She didn't want anything fancy, just a couple of sandwiches, some lunch-box drinks, a couple of apples, and a bag of chips. Not wanting to carry her purse; she put her cell phone, ID, and house key in one of Darla's back pack pockets along with their lunch, and away they went!

Much to her surprise, the temperature had warmed more than she had expected. Even so— she remembered one of the things her grandparents used to tell her. *'Don't let the sunshine fool you. It's still fall, or they would say, It's still winter'.* The short walk across the street landed them in the municipal park. The area was actually a huge square—well, more of a rectangle located in that particular part of the city. Their apartment building, along with two other apartment units were on one side of the street, and by taking a six to seven minute walk straight across the park grounds brought you face to face with the public Library.

It was late enough in the day to have drawn some of the senior citizens to the park. Some may have come from their church services, or may have been at their home just waiting until the warmer part of the day arrived in order to take a stroll through the park, or sit on the benches. While Casandra walked along with her daughter she was very aware of her surroundings.

She enjoyed seeing the older couples walking together holding hands. It caused her to wonder how long some of them had been married. She could sense that they were still in love with each other. There were a few who had taken their rest on park benches that were located along the side, and scattered along the inside of the park premises. No one could tell what the couples might have gone through in their lives, because they seemed so at peace sitting there enjoying the last warm breezes of autumn. Kids were riding bicycles, and she saw some college students in—what appeared to have been a study group, sitting under a tree on a big blanket.

Near the center of the park there was a professional photographer taking photos of two young ladies—at least he appeared to be a professional. The ladies were modeling some very fashionable clothing. They turned and posed one way and then another way following his directives as he snapped their pictures. She didn't know why, but all of a sudden a melancholy feeling swooped over her, and she thought, *'I hope they're not being scammed. Young girls fall for so much nowadays'.* But, then again; she realized she was thinking about herself at that age.

Darla had been watching them intensely, and tugged on her mother's sweater pleading to have her picture taken. At first Casandra thought Darla was talking about the professional photographer, but she was already digging in the backpack to get her mother's cell phone.

Chapter 5

It wasn't long before Darla was ready to eat. Casandra found them a nice spot near the circled wall surrounding the fountain in the middle of the town square. It seemed to be a good place to sit to watch all the comings and goings while they had their lunch. She pulled two sheets of hand sanitizer wipes from the container to cleanse their hands, and unfolded the paper towels she tore from the roll before she left home. She placed them on both of their laps. While they were eating their lunch, Casandra asked her daughter if she wanted to go to the library to get a new book. It was right in the same square, and it had a room where people could purchase donated new, and used books. The money from those sales went toward purchasing new computers for local elementary schools.

Hearing that caused Darla to hurry through her lunch, gulping down her sandwich and chips. Casandra put all their throw-a-ways in the brown paper bag and threw it in the circular trashcan a few steps from where they were sitting. Darla repositioned her school bag on her shoulders and stood to walk with her mother towards the library.

They were just about to mount the cement steps when someone called out Casandra's name. She turned back to see Brother Stillwater waving his hand in the air to get her attention. "Hey Sister Russell, Sister Casandra."

She froze in her tracts. Marcus picked up his pace to catch her before they mounted the steps. Casandra lifted her hand waist high, and gave a short, nervous wave. Fear struck her head-on. Her forehead began to bead with moisture, and her mouth became void of moisture. A nervous smile crowned the corner of her mouth. A somewhat winded Marcus panted out—"Well Sister Russell. Fancy meeting you here."

Casandra thought the same, but didn't voice it verbally. *What is he doing here?* Marcus continued talking. "You disappeared so quickly after service. I wanted to catch up with you to ask if you would be attending the next 'Singles' meeting. It's the first week in October you know." He didn't wait for an answer, but turned his attention to Darla. "And, how are you doing today Miss Darla? Your mom must have named you Darla because you're such a darling."

Darla smiled a big smile, and let out a giggle. Then turning his attention back to Casandra he said, "Deacon Anthony and Sister Belinda are sure doing a good job with the Singles, don't you think?" It wasn't Casandra's intent to stand there in public and carry on a conversation with a man. She couldn't come up with a negative answer fast enough to why she couldn't come to the next meeting, because if the truth be told—she really enjoyed the last meeting, and she couldn't use Darla for an excuse. "Yes, they are really tuned into what makes us feel comfortable."

Marcus looked down at his watch. "Oh *snap*, I'm running late. I have to get over to the nine to twelve year old story-time presentation. I'm the next presenter." He climbed a couple of steps, but turned back to look at Casandra. "Soo, Sister Russell. Will I be seeing you at the next meeting?" Thinking only of a way to be let out of the immediate situation, she blurted out—"Yeah, sure. I'll be there." Marcus gave her a beautiful smile that unexpectedly stirred her senses, and warmed her face. "Great, he said, I'll be looking forward to seeing you there."

When he scaled the steps, she thought about

grabbing Darla's hand and fleeing, but that would have been the second time today she used Darla as an excuse, and she owed her daughter more respect than that. Something dawned on her as she entered the main entrance of the library. *He called me Sister Russell, and he knew my daughter's name. How did he know my last name?*

———

Darla seemed to be taking her time looking through the selection of books. *What was taking her so long to decide on a book?* Casandra realized her own impatience. It probably wasn't taking her daughter any longer than it usually did to browse through the books; it's just that she was in a hurry to vacate the premises. She wasn't sure of how long the segments were for presenters of the 'Story hour', but she was pretty sure the term story hour was used lightly. She just wanted to be gone before Marcus' *gig* was over.

Darla finally chose two books: 'Ann of Green Gables', and a true life story, 'Anne Frank–the Diary of a Young Girl'. Casandra remembered reading both of those books when she was in elementary school, and to think those books were still on the suggested reading list for fourth and fifth graders today. She gave the attendant her library card, and paid the ten dollar donation fee for the two books.

Casandra knew that after their late lunch, dinner could be delayed, and it would not have to be a heavy meal. Anxious to get started on her reading, Darla quickly retreated to her bedroom. Casandra was furious with herself for saying 'yes' to Brother Marcus' inquiry. She was able to hide her feeling from her daughter, but right about now she could have kicked herself in the pants. She began to search the kitchen desperately for some kind of sweets to sooth her distraught emotions.

Finally settling on eating a peanut butter and jelly sandwich she was even more peeved with herself, but she only had herself to blame. She promised herself a week ago that when she went grocery shopping she would begin buying things to help her lose weight. She started out by not buying the usual junk foods and treats for herself. She wanted to replace her usual cookies, snacks cakes, ice cream and chips with healthier things like: apples, those mini carrot sticks, natural fruit juices and fixings for salads. The problem was that when she brought the snacks and treats for Darla's lunch and after school snack, she found herself sneaking in extras for herself.

Now she could have slapped herself. *What could I have been thinking of?* Her next thought answered her own question. *It certainly wasn't my health!* Still, if she could think of a way to get out of going to the 'Singles' meeting this upcoming week- she would. Casandra couldn't call Marcus to say she couldn't make it to the meeting because she didn't know any of his contact information—and then again, *why would she?* She thought about calling Deacon, or Belinda Campbell to ask for his number, but *no that wouldn't work either,* because then they would think she was interested in him.

The only obvious thing to do was to just not show up. *What was she going to do?* She could see if she was a petite girl, or even if she was attractive, but to herself, she was neither.

The ring-tone of her cell phone caused Casandra to look down on the kitchen table. It was her friend from church, Lucinda Brown. She reached for the phone and pushed Lucinda's photo. She hoped she wasn't calling to remind her of the 'Singles' meeting. Casandra apprehensively said hello. Lucinda's cheerful voice come bouncing through from the other end. "Hey girl, where were you off to today? I tried to catch up with you after service. Did you have to put out a fire or something?"

Casandra twisted the truth a little hoping her lie wouldn't be detectable. "No. No fire, she said, it's just that I promised Darla a lunch in the park, and a visit to the library, so she was anxious to get home and change her clothes." There she was again, putting the blame of her own fears on her daughter.

Casandra shared her afternoon with Lucinda, and Lucinda shared back. Their conversation was ending, and all seemed well until the question of the 'Singles' meeting finally came up. Casandra really didn't want to tell another lie—it was becoming such a habit lately, and she hated doing it.

She knew lying was a part of her pessimistic outlook on life. She originally thought it would be a way of protecting herself from life's disappointments. But now, she was involving her daughter in her lies, and if she kept it up it could involve Brother Stillwater as well. *The worst thing would be* she thought, *is if he had a chance to speak with Lucinda during the week, and told her that I told him I was coming to the meeting.* So, Casandra resolved to forcing out a somewhat mundane "yes, I'll be there." After she hung up the phone she wondered about her childish thought… *Why would Lucinda be talking with Brother Stillwater anyway?*

Chapter 6

Casandra walked Darla down to the youth corridor, and saw that she got in the right room for her age group. Several meetings took place on Wednesday evenings at Restoration of Hope Christian Ministries. There was the usual mid-week prayer meeting and Bible study held in the sanctuary, the 'Singles' meeting held in the Fellowship Hall, and the different youth meetings held in various Sunday school class rooms.

With her daughter safely in the class Casandra crept reluctantly towards the Fellowship Hall. She took a mental note of her attire. Although she never went all out for the latest *fads*, or tried to be a *fashionista,*—given the fact that most of those styles were designed for the teenagers and young *skinny* people, she was usually tasteful in her attire. Twenty-eight was by no means old, but she was a divorced woman with a nine year old daughter. She didn't want to look ridiculous trying to wear every new thing being marketed on social media, and in the fashion magazines.

There were still a lot of cute fashions out there for the slightly plus-sized lady, so she wasn't about to squeeze her size 18w body into Misses sizes 14's and 16's just to have men notice her more.

The sound of quick walking footsteps, and a lady's voice echoed behind her. "Wait up San." It was Lucinda. Casandra stopped walking to give her friend a chance to catch up to her. She was thinking it wasn't like Lucinda to be late for a meeting. She thought she would have already been in the Fellowship Hall. When her friend caught up to her, she was somewhat winded. She explained that her mother had a flat tire, so she had to go by her house to pick her up for Bible study. She said it put her behind schedule a little, but she didn't mind doing a favor for her mom.

The lady's walked in the meeting together. Casandra was glad she didn't have to walk in alone, but out of nowhere she began comparing her plus sized body to her friend's size 10, and wondered if everyone else was doing the same. She immediately reprimanded herself, because she knew that was the trick of the *enemy*.

———

Marcus knew he was out of order for thinking the thought that ran through his mind, but it was too late to draw it back. Once you think something; it's already out there. He wished *Praise and Worship* hadn't lasted as long as it did. He wanted it to end, because his mind was on attending the meeting, and seeing Sister Russell. Being the lead musician, he knew he was obligated to stay for as long as the *Spirit* was flowing and Pastor Henrietta Hastings needed him. She knew Marcus was a pivotal part of the 'Singles' ministry, so he was usually excused right after the main Praise and Worship part of service was over. The other musicians remained in place just in case they were needed, and Marcus would always try to get back before Bible Study ended to help close out the service.

Marcus tipped out of the side door near the musicians seating area. He went through the choir rehearsal room, and across the corridor to the Fellowship Hall. He knew the meeting had been going on for about twenty minutes. Marcus didn't like to come in late, but it couldn't be helped. He scanned the room hoping to find a seat where he could make eye contact with Sister Russell every now and then.

It seemed to him she rarely looked anyone directly in their face—at least not long enough to make good eye contact. He didn't know why, because to him she had beautiful eyes, and he was determined to catch their attention.

When he came in Deacon Campbell and his wife were addressing the group. They were announcing the Community event planned for the church was the upcoming Harvest Festival. They were encouraging as many singles as possible to participate in the activity. The suggestion was for the 'Singles' to handle most of the activity booths—that way it would free up some of the men and the parents to share in activities with their children. Sister Campbell said she was aware that there were a few Single parents in the group, and if they wanted to be excused from manning a booth they could. She also suggested that if they had older siblings, a grandparent, or an Aunt or Uncle who could be with their child while they attended to a booth it would be helpful.

The church grounds and parking lots covered

about two acres of land. It wasn't the larger lot area that most churches had, but it served the purposes for Restoration of Hope. Darla was nine years old and was responsible enough to hang out with her school friends for a little while. The rest of the time her sister and brother-in-law would keep an eye on her. If Casandra used Darla for an excuse why she couldn't volunteer to take charge of a booth that meant she would have to be with her for most of the day. She didn't want to embarrass Darla by trailing around behind her all afternoon as if she were a baby, so she volunteered to man a booth.

Restoration of Hope didn't encourage supporting the Halloween celebration. The church chose to support a more biblical view of the season by celebration the 'Harvest'. The Harvest Festival allowed all ministries in the church to get involved in the community outreach affair. The men took care of the fish fry and corn boil. The Women's group baked cakes and pies for the 'Cake Walk'. The young adults took care of the sweets like: cookies, brownies, cupcakes, rice crispy treats, and candy apples (which their parents would probably make anyway). The children were responsible for bringing bags of candy for the 'Grab as much as you can' event. The Food Pantry would give away food boxes to the needy, and the Wisdom Ministry donated the apples for the 'Bobbing for Apples' contest, took care of the snack, hotdog, and soda booths. All in all, the church was looking forward to a great Community Outreach event.

Chapter 7

The morning of the Harvest Community event was somewhat crisp—yet sunny and bright. Anthony and Antoinette said they would keep an eye on Darla, and have her to check in with them every so often. They didn't want to crowd her being as they had a small child of their own to look after.

At the time Casandra volunteered she had no idea that Deacon and Sister Campbell were planning to have two Singles to work a booth together. Their reasoning was to get them to venture out beyond their normal circle of friends. They weren't trying to play matchmaker, because most of the Singles in the Ministry were females anyway. But, having kept their eyes open for possible relationships, they had a pretty good idea if a certain gentleman's interest floated toward a certain lady.

So, a few days before the event Deacon Campbell called Brother Stillwater to say he and his wife were grouping two 'Singles' to a booth. He said he didn't have a second person to share the booth with Sister Casandra Russell, and wanted to know if he wouldn't mind being her partner. Marcus tried not to voice his enthusiasm, but jumped at the chance. The 'Ring Toss' game was added at the last minute, and was assigned to Casandra's booth. Since she was one of the two volunteers left who didn't have a partner, *fate*–(with a little nudge from the Campbell's) took *her* assignment to bring the two of them together.

———

Casandra was trying her best to find something appropriate to ware to the festival. She didn't own a lot of dress-down, everyday casual clothes mainly because most of her wardrobe consisted of *dressy-casual* for work, and the other part was what she wore to church—basically the two main places she spent most of her time when out of the apartment. She didn't care much for jeans anyway because they caused her things to rub together, and they also emphasized her hips and rear end. She had clothes she wore when she worked around the house to vacuum and clean-up, but she wouldn't dare wear those frumpy things in public.

She looked through her closet again hoping to find something that would suffice, and wishing she had thought of the pending situation earlier in the week. The pant suits she wore to work were too dressy, and she always put on pantyhose, or a knee length panty liner with those. *No way,* she thought *am I going to walk around all day with all that stuff on.*

Darla tapped on her mother's bedroom door. "Are you ready yet mommy?" "Almost honey", Casandra responded back, although she knew she was nowhere close to being ready. She quickly checked the time on her cellphone. She was running a little behind, but she wasn't late. Her guess was that her daughter was excited about the festival and was anxious to get the day started.

The volunteers had to be at church early to set up their booths, so she let Darla know she was going to be dropping her off at her Auntie's house to wait until the Harvest Festival got started. She knew her daughter was okay with that, but Darla just wanted to get going.

While Casandra tried to resolve her apparel dilemma, she reminded her daughter of a couple of Saturday chores that needed to be done around the house before they left. Since the weather would probably start out cool in the morning, she decided on a summer *'cow-neck'* sweater, and a pair of casual slacks—although she still was going to wear panty hose. Casandra wasn't sure of how much walking she would have to do, or how long she would have to stand attending her booth, so she decided to put on her good tennis shoes.

———

Belinda Campbell scurried back and forth across the parking lot between the different booths her ministry was in charge of. She wanted to be sure every booth was set up with a table, two folding chairs, the equipment to play their game, and the prizes for the winners. Other church members were overseeing activities like the 'Bobbing for Apples', the 'Cake Walk', the pie eating contest, and the arts and crafts. The men had the fryers going for the fish-fry, and the pots for the corn boil. Their signs were posted for the cost of a dinner, or for just a fish sandwich.

A rented *'Bouncy-Castle'* was set up on the small playground to attract the little children. Some of the other games in the children's area were the three-legged sack race, the bowling pin game, and the egg walk, or better said the egg race. Belinda looked up to see cars turning into the church parking lot. She hoped they were the helpers, and not patrons ready for the festival to start.

Everything seemed to be going according to schedule as far as she knew, but that was only from her perspective. Looking around, Belinda hoped some of her 'Singles' were the ones turning onto the church lot because one of her booths was shy of a partner, and another was completely empty.

Deacon Campbell came from across the field to meet his wife. He was carrying several orange rubber caution-cones that were to be placed on the playground, and had three stop-watches hanging on long cords around his neck. He said the stop-watches were for a couple of the racing games, and for the pie eating contest.

Casandra dropped Darla off at her sister's house, and headed towards the church. She was excited about participating in an activity at the church. She attended service every Sunday, went to Bible study when she could, and now attended the

'Singles' meetings once a month.

In thinking of that, a slight smile lit her face. She guessed it was because she was giving herself *praise* for getting more involved in church activities. *Besides,* she thought, *I need to set a better example for Darla.*

Casandra parked her car in the area designated for the festival workers and church staff. She gave herself a quick face-check in the rear view mirror, and got out of the car. Standing there, she thought the best thing to do was to look for Deacon, or Sister Campbell. Surveying the area she realized that what were deemed as *booths* were separated areas that had eight to ten feet length tables in them. However; there were several spots that had small tents set up for some of the other activities. She wasn't sure if they personally belonged to individual members, or if they were rented. None-the-less, it made the area look more like a festival.

The Women's Auxiliary was sorting out signs and taping them to tables, and on the sides of the tents. Casandra read a few of the signs, but that didn't help her much, because she had no idea which game booth she was assigned to. She had to find someone with a list of booth assignments, and most likely that would be Sister Campbell.

Casandra stood still and began to look around. She turned her eyes to the left, and then to the right— no Sister Campbell. It wasn't until she turned her body to face the playground area that she spotted her standing next to her husband. Casandra began to walk in that direction waving her hand in the air, and calling her name as she went.

———

Marcus Stillwater sent a quiet rebuke to himself for the excitement he was feeling over sharing a booth with Casandra Russell. He knew he was beginning to have fond thoughts of her, but he knew that didn't mean she felt the same way about him. As a matter of fact when he thought about it, she was rather stand-offish. Marcus could only hope that today her attitude toward him would be more receptive. He told himself to focus on the spiritual significance of the community outreach event, and since he would be sharing a booth with Casandra he cautioned his body members to do the same.

He thought back on the Sunday afternoon he saw Casandra and Darla at the library. He was hoping they would have finished their book search in time to sit in on his reading secession with the kids, but they never showed up. He was disappointed, because he thought that was a chance for him to win her attention.

Marcus arrived at Restoration of Hope, and parked his SUV in the designated area for the volunteer help. He cleared the front passenger seat of a few personal items, and removed his satchel of music from the floor behind the driver's seat. He put everything in the trunk, and pushed the 'lock' button on the remote key fob. He reasoned there would be many community folk coming to the festival, and all of them were not *'church-goers'*. So, no use inviting trouble. Marcus said a short prayer asking God to make his meeting with Casandra go easy, and prayed she wouldn't be too uncomfortable working around him.

He began searching his mind for pleasant, ice-breaker chats to start conversation with her when he heard a distant voice echo his name. He looked up to see Deacon Campbell coming his way carrying a large box, while maneuvering a sign and several other things. Marcus ran to his aid relieving his arms of the box to the smile and 'thank you' of Deacon Campbell. "Thank you Brother Stillwater. I was just headed to your booth. I was doubling up

on things to bring this way so I wouldn't have to make two trips, and found myself overloaded."
"Not a problem, Marcus replied, which way are we headed?" Deacon Campbell nodded his head to the left and said, "Right up there on the left under that tent. That's where you and your booth partner will be."

Marcus was surprised that he and Casandra's booth was actually under a tent. Two rectangle tables were set up side by side in the middle of the tent. There were two medal folding chairs at a distance behind the tables, and two more up front that were placed on either side of the tent at the entrance. Marcus set the large box on the table, and began to empty its contents.

Deacon Campbell explained that the tent belonged to him and Sister Campbell. He said they used it from time to time at family gatherings, and church events. He said when he and his wife thought of the type of game he and Sister Russell would be manning, they thought a more closed-in environment would be best. That way they wouldn't have to chase missed throws so far; especially if it got too warm, or even too windy. He didn't mention that he and his wife were also playing a little bit of a *matchmaker*.

Marcus had just emptied out the last contents of the box, and was pondering over how to arrange the empty soda bottles when Sister Campbell entered the tent followed by Casandra.

Chapter 8

Casandra was thrown off guard to see Marcus standing in the tent next to Deacon Campbell. *Was he there just to help with the festival? Could he have been working with the men?* She couldn't by no stretch of the imagination—guess they were to be booth partners. *Surely the Campbell's would not have assigned male and female Singles to work in a booth as partners.* Casandra came out of her pondering just in time to hear her worst fear. The Campbell's were introducing them as booth partners for the festival.

She couldn't believe what she was hearing! She felt an immediate terror whelm up inside of her, and her first notion was to run as fast as she could. But, for some odd reason her legs wouldn't move. In her mind she could see herself fleeing– but she was still there. *What was she going to do?*

Marcus gave himself a gentle reminder of his promise to act as normal as he could when he met face to face with his booth partner. He moved slowly from the other side of the table with his hand extended to greet Casandra. Belinda Campbell noticed the hesitant look on Casandra's face, and spoke up quickly in a joyful voice. "Casandra, I don't know if you've ever had the pleasure of meeting our church musician before, but he is a very gifted individual. His talents reach far beyond his musical abilities displayed on Sunday mornings." By that time Marcus was in front of her shaking her partially extended hand— although she wasn't aware of how it came to be in that position. His mellow voice first addressed Sister Campbell. "Please, Sister Campbell you're too kind", and then to Casandra. "It's a pleasure to meet you again Miss Russell." Marcus released her hand, but she could still feel the strong—yet gentle grip with which he embraced it.

Belinda Campbell interrupted. "*Again?*" she said. "So you two have already been acquainted?" Casandra wished that Marcus had not said 'to *see you again*'. She felt very uncomfortable by the way he injected that. Marcus was continuing on and said, "Yes, well not exactly acquainted, but we have met. It was a couple of Sundays ago at the Library. We sort of bumped in to each other"

Casandra didn't want the Campbell's to get the wrong idea, so she jumped in with an explanation to fix the situation. "Well it was all accidental. I was taking my daughter for a Sunday afternoon *backpack* lunch at the square, and then we decided to go to the library. It just so happened that Brother Marcus was there at the same time–to ahh, do a reading secession with a group of kids, and we happened upon each other." *Happened upon each other. Where did that old phrase come from?* Casandra sensed that she was beginning to ramble on, so she stopped talking.

Deacon Campbell thought the prolonged silence following Casandra's abrupt halt was a bit awkward, so rubbing his hands together, and then clapping them in mid-air, he said "Okay. Let us leave you two young folk alone so you can set up your game booth, and we (giving his wife a raised eyebrow) will scurry on to see that all the other stations are ready, and set to go." He explained how they were to handle the game tickets; wished them good luck, and departed. Outside the tent Anthony Campbell reached for his wife's hand, and gave it a gentle squeeze. They didn't look back, but they both could feel that Marcus and Casandra's eyes were starring them in the back.

Antoinette grabbed a pair of sunglasses, BJ's light jacket, her sweater and her husband's baseball cap. With the early October weather being so 'iffy', she wasn't sure of what she would need later on. Her husband had gone to back the car out of the garage, and Darla was right on her uncle's heels. She was so excited about getting to the festival one would think she had a booth to attend to. Her mother dropped her off earlier that morning, but the forty-five minutes Darla had to wait seemed more like an hour and a half to Antoinette, because her niece asked her every five minutes or so—if it was time to go yet!

Darla lifted BJ from his stroller and helped him into his car seat. She was an only child, so she enjoyed the feeling of being a big sister to her almost three year old nephew. She secured the three-way interlocking fastener on the toddler's seat, and gave him one of his toys. Anthony held the front passenger door open until his wife was seated, and then went around to the driver's side and hopped in. Darla sat across from her nephew in the back seat and fastened herself in her safety belt. Anthony cheerfully asked if all were ready to go. A round of *'yeses'* came from everybody. "Then, it's off to the festival we go" he said.

———

Marcus and Casandra stood without moving for a few awkward moments. Then Marcus broke the silence by saying, "Well, it looks like we're booth partners." "Yes, I guess so" she said, reluctantly smiling. Marcus moved back to the other side of the tables where he was standing before the threesome had arrived. Timidly, he looked at Casandra and said, "Okay Sister Russell what say we get this game set up before people start arriving." "Oh, you don't have to call me 'Sister' Russell. I mean…Casandra will be alright."

The introvert in her really wanted to comply with the formality of the estranged relationship for the main purpose of not becoming too familiar with him, but for the life of her, she drew a blank, and couldn't remember his last name, so to stay on a formal basis seemed futile. The only thing she could remember about his last name was that it sounded *'Native American'*. "Alright then— Casandra it is!"

Marcus asked if she had any idea of how they should set up the *'Ring Toss'* game. He said it had been a while since he had been to a carnival, and he was trying to remember how the soda pop bottles were supposed to be arranged. Casandra thought the bottles were supposed to be set up in a triangular fashion, but she wasn't sure if the narrow end of the triangle was supposed to facing out toward them, or away from them.

They tried it her way, however there was something that just didn't look right about it. Marcus asked if she could remember what the game looked like from the last time she took her daughter to a carnival. Casandra was a little embarrassed, and desperately tried to visualize the game, but the truth of the matter was the last two times she was even near a Carnival was when she was visiting her grandparents, and they took Darla to the Carnival. She took a break from parenting while she and her cousin spent the day shopping and going to the movies.

The twosome stood back to observe the table. Each of them took a Toss ring in their hand and threw it towards the bottles. Neither of their tosses landed a *'ringer'*. They concluded the bottles could have been set up too closely together. Just when they were going to widen the space between the bottles, it dawned on Casandra that the formation was wrong. The bottles were supposed to be lined up in a square, or rectangular pattern.

The different color bottles were supposed to be set in a spot that was most challenging to *'ring'* and were worth the bigger prize.

They rearranged the soda bottles, and tried their tosses again. Neither of them 'ringed' a bottle, but at least they knew they were on the right track. Marcus suggested a few more practice throws, and his toss 'ringed' two bottles. However, Casandra's tosses missed the targets completely with one of them landing between the bottles, and the other on the ground. Coming to her aid Marcus retrieved the tossed ring, and hurried back to the table. "Here, he said, let's try your tosses again, but this time I'll try to guide your hand." Without even thinking about what he was doing, he stood in back of Casandra, and put the 'Ring' in her right hand. Casandra stood there in motionless shock. She was too afraid to speak, and certainly too petrified to move.

Marcus still unaware of his presumptuous position continued to aid in instructing her tossing skills. "You are right handed I aren't you?" All she could do was nod her head indicating a *yes*. Marcus proceeded to lift her right arm, and leaning in closer lined up Casandra's hand with his own. Her hand began to tremble, and that's when he realized he had overstepped the bounds of personal social distancing. Coming to himself, he quickly released her hand and moved aside. "I apologize. That was so stupid of me. I did that without thinking. I guess I was a bit anxious to help you *ring* a toss." Blushing, and still reeling from his closeness, Casandra accepted his apology. Marcus was embarrassed for what had just happened, but he knew within his heart he didn't regret standing that close to her.

Chapter 9

Walking slightly ahead of her husband and Darla, Antoinette caught the short scene between her sister, and the handsome church musician. She slowed her pace, and looked behind her to be sure her niece was not at her heels. Darla lagged a few yards behind—her focus still on being the 'aunty' to BJ for the moment, but Antoinette had a feeling that would soon fade once the festival got under way.

Antoinette gave a much louder than needed greeting as she approached the tent. "Hello. Hey, you guys under the tent." Casandra turned when she recognized her sister's voice. Antoinette was waving her arm in the air. Her designer sunglasses hid the questionable look in her eyes as she kept a smile on her face.

The foursome reached the booth, and Darla ran to give her mother a big hug. Casandra began introducing her family to her booth partner—

although she was sure they knew each other from church services—still a formal introduction was not out of order. The two men greeted each other with a handshake, and a *"what's up"*. Darla recognized Marcus as the churches' musician, but then commented aloud she remembered seeing him at the library. Immediately a flush of embarrassment returned to Casandra's face—though she didn't know why. Marcus shook Antoinette's hand, and said he had seen her at church, but he didn't know she and Sister Russell were sisters.

Darla did something next that caused her mother to cringe, but to a child may have seemed like a normal thing to do. Although Casandra had taken care in seeing that her daughter had ample money to spend at the festival, and was sure if something came up where her daughter needed more money she was certain that her sister and brother-in-law would handle it; even if she had to pay them back later. Nevertheless—out of the *blue,* Darla said, "Mommy can I have a little more money to spend?"

Casandra was shocked, and she wasn't the only one. Antoinette couldn't believe her ears. Casandra (in a quiet like manner) respectfully reminded her daughter that she had given her ample funds to participate in many activities and have a full day of food and fun. "But Mommy, what if I spend all my money and then see something else I want to do?" "Then you'll just have to be careful of how you spend your money won't you?" She was trying not to speak through clenched teeth.

Marcus knew this was a private affair between mother and daughter—yet he also saw it as an opportunity for him to make a friendly gestor. "How 'bout if I add…let's say, five dollars to what you have?" Darla's face lit up. Casandra broke in (a little too loudly) "**No, no**. That won't be necessary. I appreciate your gestor, but I think ten dollars is more than enough for a nine year old to spend at a community festival. And, if I know my sister; and I'm sure I do, she's probably already added to her niece's funds." She shoot a discerning eye at Antoinette who quickly looked the other way.

Marcus felt a little out of place because he had already removed the money from his wallet. He had to think of something fast. He took a few steps forward holding the money in the air. He looked at Casandra's face which he was unable to clearly discern, and looked on Darla's disappointed face, which he could very clearly discern. Trying to amend the situation he said, "Oh, this isn't free money. You have to earn it." "Earn it!" Darla exclaimed. "Yes, he said, now this is the deal."

Marcus glanced over at Casandra, and was pleased that her expression had soften a little, but still was curious. He walked over to Anthony and gave the money to him (knowing to involve and show respect to the male dynamic in their family), "I'm going to give your uncle the money to hold for you, and if you really, really need it, I'm sure he'll make the right decision for you." Marcus gave an understanding wink at Anthony. "The rest of the deal, he continued, is that when the festival is over, you have to come back to your mother's booth and help us pack up our things."

Darla looked from face to face acting like she was thinking the deal over, but the adults knew she wasn't about to turn down another five dollars. "Um okay, she said, it's a deal. She extended her hand toward Marcus for a shake. He accepted, and resolutely gave the nine year old's hand a firm shake. All the adults had a good laugh, and the foursome left the tent, once again leaving Marcus and Casandra alone.

The Campbell's spent their time monitoring the 'Singles'. They went from station to station checking on them, and manning their booths for needed breaks. The breaks allowed them to go inside the air conditioned building to use the restrooms, get a cold drink, and much to their surprise partake of the food buffet that was prepared for the workers in the Fellowship Hall. It was Pastor's Hastings way of thanking everyone for their volunteer services.

When the Campbell's came to relieve Marcus and Casandra the twosome thanked them again for the use of their tent. Marcus and Casandra walked across the parking lot, and down to one of the back entry doors of the church that lead into the Fellowship Hall. He stepped aside and held the door open so Casandra could enter before him. It almost caught her off guard. She'd been so used to opening her own doors, or working with guys at the office who seldom held the door open for a lady. She should have expected a man like Brother Stillwater to open doors for ladies. It fit his gentlemanly character.

The cool air swooped their faces, and both of

them let out a sigh of relief at the same time. They chuckled, and Marcus said, "I guess we didn't realize that in the South the beginning of October could still be quite warm." "Yeah, the sun was shining, but I guess I got used to it." "Okay Sister Russ…, I mean Casandra, let's say we freshen up and meet back here in five minutes. Casandra walked across the hall to the ladies room thinking: *Now I wish I would have left well enough alone, and let him call me Sister Russell, because every time his melodiously smooth voice says 'Casandra' I get a fluttering in my stomach.*

Casandra took care of personal matters, and ran a paper towel under cold water. She dabbed her face, and the back of her neck. On her way back across the Hall she began to feel nervous and tense. She had just begun to feel comfortable talking with Brother Marcus in the tent—*but what are people going to think when they see us sitting with each other at the same table in the Fellowship Hall?* The old widowers, and church mothers were always keeping their eyes peeled on Singles trying to play 'match-maker'. She peeped in one side of the double door window pane. Sure enough, Marcus was sitting alone at a table waiting for her. She took a deep breath, and pushed the door open. Marcus stood when she entered the room. He wanted to deploy his chivalrous mannerism again, by holding her chair for her, but in a situation like this, not knowing where she was going to sit he thought it would be a bit much, so he just stayed put. A pleasant smile cornered his mouth when she decided to sit directly across from him.

There was an entire smorgasbord of food prepared for the workers. If she had been by herself, she probably would have filled two plates, but sense she was with a man, and they only had ten more minutes of their break Casandra got a can of root beer soda, a grilled burger from the aluminum warming pan, and took a little lettuce and tomato for her bun. If this had been any other occasion, and she had been alone, she would have loaded her burger with onion. She loved onions. But, considering she had to go back to the tent and work in close proximity with Marcus–she passed on the onions.

Before they left the table Casandra thanked Marcus for the way he handled giving Darla the extra five dollars. She said she believed that after doing her expected chores around the apartment, and giving her a little *just because'* money—she had to earn anything that was over and above that. Marcus knew the way he ended up handling the situation the way he did was because of the tenseness he saw on Casandra's face, but he didn't tell her that. He just smiled and nodded a *thank you.* On the way back to tent he smiled to himself thinking; *I liked the way Casandra phrased her beliefs and opinion without coming across in an offensive manner.*

The rest of the afternoon was moving along smoothly. Their booth had a lot of activity, and they collected over thirty dollars' worth of game tickets. The tickets cost a dollar each, and it took two tickets to play the 'Ring-Toss' game. Even though they were captains over the game, they paid for the games they played keeping score of the better player. They opened up to some small chit-chat whenever they were alone in the booth. It wasn't full-fledged conversations, or anything too personal, but they did pick up little tidbits of information about each other.

Casandra was surprised when Mr. Williams (the afterschool tutor) from Darla's school stopped by the booth. He said he wasn't much on playing carnival and festival games, but he was for supporting the community. He tried his hand at one game, and donated the rest of the five dollars to financially help the event.

Just before it was time for their second break, Lucinda ran up to the booth. She was already making insinuating eye stares at her friend. "Hello Brother Stillwater. When I came back from my first break and saw you and 'Sandra leaving for yours, I was so happy that you guys were sharing a booth *together*." "Oh, he said rather flatly, and why is that?" Casandra was darting stern rolling eyeballs at Lucinda. "Oh, I don't know—no real reason in particular, she said weakly. Just happy I guess...that is...I mean that all of us 'Singles' have booth partners." Her voice trailed off. Lucinda looked at the confused look on Marcus' face, and the expression on Casandra's. "I—I guess I'll see you later San. Bye." With that she quickly skirted out of the tent being very aware of how much she had just embarrassed herself, and her friend.

The church festival was to be over at five o'clock, and it was nearly three o'clock before the Campbell's got back to their booth to relieve them for their second break. Deacon Campbell told them the breaks were now extended to twenty minutes. Sister Belinda told Casandra she saw Darla and the rest of her family in the Choir room about thirty minutes ago. That's where the 'Cake Walk' was being held. She said she wasn't sure if she had won anything yet because she was still in line holding her tickets.

Casandra knew her daughter quite well, and if her persistent nature followed through, she was mighty sure Darla would keep trying over and over again until she won something. The Cake Walk entry was three tickets a piece. That would cost Darla three dollars every time she tried.

Walking toward the building; not only was Casandra worried, but a little angry too. Now that Darla had extra money her thoughts went to the money Marcus gave to Anthony. She probably wouldn't stop trying until she won a cake, or brownies, or whatever it took to come away with a prize. She didn't want Darla to spend all of her money on sweets. She hoped she would save a little back for her church offering. All of a sudden she found herself putting the blame on *Brother* Stillwater. *Yes, that's his last name...*Stillwater.

Opening the door for Casandra, Marcus noticed what appeared to be a concern look on her face. "Is everything alright?" Stepping from the outside into the air conditioned building cold air swished her face. "Oh yes. I was just thinking about... well it doesn't matter. It was really nothing." After all what was she going to say: *My daughter is probably coming home with a big, fat cake that I most likely will eat a good portion of before going to bed, and it'll be all your fault!*

The two of them agreed to follow the same routine they had done on their first break, except this time the break was longer. Marcus politely asked if he could get anything for her in the way of refreshments when he got his. Casandra felt a little *huff* rise up in her spirit, but pushed it back and told him she wouldn't be long, that she would look things over when she got back.

Casandra was peeved with herself about the familiar defenses that floated back so easily. She entered the ladies room with feelings running ramped through her mind. *I don't want Brother Stillwater, or any other man for that matter caring about my thoughts. I have made up my mind years ago to live happily single with my daughter.* Leaving the ladies room the huff in her attitude continued. *And what gives him the right to think that all women take a long time in the restroom?*

She tried to push past the remaining fifteen minutes of their break. Casandra tried to make herself listen to Marcus' comments. She plastered a fake smile on her face, and nodded her head every now and then, but he must have felt the sudden disinterest. Marcus was a good, kind gentleman, but she couldn't let his seemingly attraction to her pull her defenses down. Her façade was her covering.

Stepping back outside into the October surroundings Casandra viewed the trees with their many colors of gold, red, yellow, and orange. She quietly thought to herself as she walked back to the booth with Marcus Stillwater—*yes, I guess I'm like the season of Autumn; strutting brightly gay colors of happiness on the surface, and slowly dying underneath.*

Chapter 10

Darla was all smiles as she ran toward the tent. Her uncle was carrying a covered tray of fudge nut brownies as he balanced a three layer lemon cake with butter-cream frosting. "Look, look Mommy. Look at what I won in the Cake-Walk. Darla wanted to share everything about her day right then, however her uncle and aunt were happy for the suggestion Brother Stillwater made earlier for her to return to the tent to help her mother clean up.

They enjoyed the festival, but they were not teenagers. Keeping an eye on a nine year old and her friends plus pushing a toddler around all day in a stroller took a toll on their energy. They were anxious to get home, give BJ a bath, and prepare for Sunday so they could rest for the remainder of the day.

Anthony had planned to take the cake and brownies to Casandra's car, and then walk back to the far side of the church's parking lot to where his vehicle was parked, but Marcus suggested for him to leave the goodies in the tent, and he would carry them to Casandra's car when they left. He said it wouldn't be any trouble because all the volunteers had a reserved parking area, and he was sure that her car wouldn't be far from his.

Casandra hugged and kissed her sister, nephew, and her brother-in-law. She fought past the unwarranted feeling she now had toward Marcus, and tried to stifle the newest add on. *I don't need him to help me to my car with anything. Who said I needed help anyway? I wouldn't have that much to carry if he hadn't given her the extra money!* Marcus could sense that something had shifted in Casandra's attitude towards him—not that she had warmed up to him completely in the first place, but he did think he had made some headway. Now, things appeared to have taken a few steps backward. He felt an apparent decline in the short lived connection.

Darla was bursting to share her day with her mother, so to give them some alone time Marcus collected all the tickets, the cash money, and the pad they used to record how many games were played. He gathered the rest of the left over prizes, and decided to turn everything in to save time. He felt uncomfortable using Darla as bait, but he had to try to regain ground with her mother. Before he left the tent he turned to her and said; "I'll be back in a few minutes, so don't you and your mother go running off with those goodies. I'll carry them to the car for you—besides, I love brownies, and I hope you'll let me have one, (a dazzling smile followed his remark) so help your mother put the soda bottles, and the ring tosses in those boxes. Your mom will show you how to do it."

There he goes again, Casandra thought, *it's as if he was reading my mind. I was going to do that very thing— except I probably would have had to pass him when he was on the way back to the tent before I got to my car.* Casandra put a leer on her face reasoning that was the silliest plan she had ever thought of. She knew it was her way of trying to avoid more conversation with him. Not only would it have been downright rude to leave, but immature as well. After all she had to come to church the next day, and what excuse could she have given him then. Besides, Darla–who seemed to be taking a liking to this stranger would have laced her with a thousand questions why they left.

Casandra and Darla were putting the last of the bottles in the box when Darla told her mother she won the prizes in the Cake Walk with the five dollars Mr. Stillwater had given her. She said Uncle Anthony stood on the sideline just in case she needed the extra money. Casandra tried to think positively about her daughter's excitement, and mustered out a "that's nice honey", but thought— *sure, why not? He wants to keep me overweight and unattractive!* She knew that wasn't true, and wanted to kick herself for thinking it. She knew it wasn't fair, and it certainly wasn't his character.

A familiar voice interrupted her musing. It was Lucinda's. She spoke to Darla and asked her how she enjoyed the festival. Without really waiting for her answer, she beckoned for her friend to step outside of the tent. "'Sandra, please except my apology. I feel so awful. Whatever I was thinking in my head must have just popped out of my mouth. I'm so sorry I embarrassed you. I guess I embarrassed myself too. Please forgive me." "Well, to tell you the truth, I was almost speechless and very much embarrassed, but I accept your apology."

Lucinda looked over her shoulder and saw Marcus approaching the tent. She quickly said she would see her friend in church, and not wanting to cross paths with Marcus again she scurried around to the back side of the tent, and disappeared.

Marcus felt somewhat awkward when he entered the tent. There was a certain amount of tenseness in the air—though not between the two of them. It must have been the sight of Lucinda fleeing in *humiliation*. All of a sudden both of them-seemingly knowing his thoughts, released a low grade chuckle that built itself in to a robust of laughter. Darla asked them what was so funny. "Oh, nothing Brother Marcus said, it's just that God is giving us joy at the end of a successful day's event."

He told Casandra that when he went to turn in their tickets the Campbell's let him know they were to leave the box on the tables, and the 'break-down' crew would be by to disassemble everything.

Marcus and Darla followed Casandra to the church to get her purse, and then went on to where their vehicles were parked. Casandra should have guessed that her daughter was going to bring up how she won the desserts. Darla told Marcus that it was his five dollars that allowed her to purchase enough tickets to win the two prizes.

When they reached her car Casandra put the tray of brownies on the floor in back of her seat. Marcus was holding the cake in one hand, and the

driver door open for her with the other. Darla
hopped in the front passenger seat, and fastened
her safety belt. When Casandra was settled in her
seat, Marcus handed her the cake, and she passed it
over to her daughter; cautioning her to hold the
cake plate with both hands, and to be very careful.

Marcus; still holding the door ajar peeked his
head in the car, and looking at Darla said, "I am
glad I was a help in you winning those prizes in the
Cake Walk. Now, I do hope I'll get a chance to
sample some of those delicious goodies." "Oh
yes", she began excitedly, but before her daughter
said something rash—like inviting him over to
their house. Casandra interrupted her sentence.
"Yes Brother Stillwater, we'll bring you a couple of
brownies, and a large slice of cake tomorrow
morning." And having said that he closed the door.
She turned the key in the ignition, and put the gear
in reverse without saying another word.

Chapter 11

Casandra carried the cake and her purse up the steps to their apartment while Darla followed with the container of brownies. On the ride home Darla chatted away about meeting up with a couple of her school friends and what they did together as a threesome. She said each of them had to check back in with an adult they came with every half hour, so they went together as a group to whoever they checked in with. She said Aunti Naa Net (the name she called her since she was about two years old) told her that was a good idea for all of them to stay together as a group whenever they checked in, that way all the adults could vouch for them at any given time.

They put the goodies on the kitchen table, and went to the bathroom to wash their face and hands. Darla told her mother that she and her friends came by her booth, but she and Brother Marcus were on their break. Deacon Campbell asked them if they wanted to play the game, but she told him she would wait until her mother got back.

It was only a little after five o'clock; not very late, but Casandra wanted to get their showers out of the way so she could turn her mind toward fixing something for dinner—although she supposed neither one of them were very hungry. She asked her daughter about her food intake for the day, and she was sorry she asked. Aside from cotton candy, funnel cake, popcorn, a Carmel apple, soda, and a giant pretzel, Darla had managed to slip in a hot dog and an apple-which she bobbed for, but hadn't eaten yet. Needless to say, she wasn't very hungry. With the two breaks she had taken Casandra wasn't very hungry either. On their second break some delicious macaroni shrimp salad had been set out, and she loved sea food. As a matter fact several new items graced the buffet. She scooped up a couple spoons of the pasta salad, and a few Swedish meatballs. Sitting back at the table Casandra tried to be cordial. She didn't want her irritation to surface. She just hoped Marcus couldn't see through her façaded demeanor.

Marcus drove his SUV around the slight curve in his driveway that led to the garage entrance on the side of the house. He pushed the button on the operator clipped attached to the sun visor, and moved the vehicle slowly forward. In the kitchen he dropped a few things on the medium sized island, and made his way through the master bedroom to use the facility. Marcus mulled things over in his head, and he just couldn't figure out why Casandra's behavior had cooled towards him. He came back to the kitchen, got a bottle of water from the fridge, and flopped down on the living room sofa.

He knew he should have been going over some music for Sunday's service, but there he sat thinking about Casandra. The 'Praise Team' practiced on Thursday evenings, so there wasn't much more to prepare for. He knew the basics were taken care of; still he usually would have gone to the keyboard letting his fingers trickle over the keys while he prayed and meditated on what the Spirit would give him should the hype of the service move in another direction. As a musician he not only had to be prepared for the music accompaniment expected with each service, but also be sensitive to the move of the Holy Spirit and flow along with the pastor.

Marcus' mind floated to the soft 'Cow-neck' sweater Casandra wore. He admired the way she dressed because her clothes weren't too clingy. He didn't mind that she was a little on the 'plus size', but that's what was so admirable about her. She didn't try to squeeze herself into clothes that were too small—which was not always the case with some women of weight. When he found himself wondering what she would wear to church on Sunday he knew it was time for him to move from the sofa to his music room. He had to concentrate on music–not on Sister Casandra Russell.

After her bath Darla wanted to delve into the sweets, but her mother knew she needed at least one more staple substance in her stomach. While Darla was bathing Casandra had fixed a small portion of sliced hot dogs and baked beans for her to eat. When she finished eating, Casandra allowed her daughter to have two brownies. Darla took her dessert to her bedroom. She had already begun planning what she wanted to wear to church, and she searched for the rest of her needed ensemble. She and her two friends planned to dress alike on Sunday—or at least come as closely as they could to look like a threesome.

Casandra usually let her daughter wear whatever she selected as long as it wasn't too outlandish; which really wasn't a problem because she didn't buy Darla those types of clothes. She by no means had a bland wardrobe, just nothing too 'fad-ish' or things that were too mature for a nine year old girl to wear. Besides, some of what the market advertised as 'popular' was definitely out of Casandra's price range, and her daughter's age group. Darla (running into complications) told her mother what she was trying to do, and Casandra was only too glad to help her ramble through her closet for the perfect outfit.

After Darla was happy and settled, Casandra went back to the kitchen to clean up for the night. There wasn't much to do having only fixed hot dogs, baked beans, and a side bowl of salad. Now, alone with her thoughts the three layered lemon cake became very tempting. It seemed like it was calling her name–drawing her in to cut a slice, or two, or three! Moving quickly to avert the temptation the next thing that happened was very strange.

A verses, or part of a verse from the Bible came to her mind. *"Say not when you are tempted, I am tempted of God…"* She couldn't remember the rest of the verse, but she smiled to herself that something like that came to her thoughts at all. She reached in the top cabinet above the sink and took out the plastic cake carrier. It would be good for Darla in the morning to find that her cake had not been delved in to. Casandra knew it would make her daughter feel mighty special if she could cut the first piece for Brother Stillwater; *although she didn't know why she thought that.*

She washed the plate the cake had been on, and put it on the table. She would return it tomorrow to the Fellowship Hall where she was sure there would be a table set up for returned items such as that.

Chapter 12

Casandra had already planned in her mind what she wanted to wear to church on Sunday. The October weather was cool and crisp, but not to the point where she needed a jacket. A Cardigan sweater, or a light poncho would be enough if the weather changed, but she didn't think it would. Casandra told Darla it was alright to cut extra-large slices of cake for Brother Stillwater. She knew it was more cake than she desired for them to eat, but she didn't tell her that. She sliced one quarter of the cake, and put the large chunk on a saucer. Darla cut the chunk into three slices, and wrapped them in aluminum foil. She also put three brownies in a plastic zip closure bag, and placed it on the table.

Even though they arrived at the church earlier than usual, Darla was anxious for her mother to find a parking space. She didn't know if it was because Darla wanted to find her friends to check out their outfits, or if it was to give Brother

Stillwater the cake and brownies. Casandra's first mission was to return the cake plate to the Fellowship Hall. She parked in the south parking lot, because that was the lot closest to the Fellowship Hall doors. She was apprehensive about seeing Marcus again so soon after yesterday's event. She also knew it wouldn't be right to send Darla by herself to give him the goodies. *Why were her emotions so confused?* She wanted to see him again, but not face-to-face if that made any sense. She told herself she wanted to see him from a distance. She knew it was just so she wouldn't have to look into his eyes, or was it so he wouldn't look in hers.

There weren't many cars in the parking lot–at least not on that side of the building, but then again it was still early. When she parked the car she told Darla it was best if they find Brother Stillwater before she met up with her friends. The choir rehearsal room was directly across from the Fellowship Hall, so that way it would only take a few more steps for her to deliver the cake and brownies to Brother Stillwater. Besides, once those 5th graders met up with each other she could only surmise that delivering the package to Marcus Stillwater would end up being her responsibility anyway, and she felt better that the gesture would come from her daughter rather than from her.

———

Marcus parked his SUV in the south parking lot as he always did because that entrance door was closest to the choir room. He stood in the parking lot looking towards the spot where the game tent had been set-up for him, and Casandra just the day before. A smile lit his face remembering all the little things that made that afternoon enjoyable. He didn't know how the Campbell's ended up partnering them together as booth companions, but he surely was thankful they did. He had been looking for an opportunity to talk to Casandra, but every time he tried to approach her, she was either in a hurry to get somewhere, or she was already gone.

Brother Stillwater entered the church hoping that the choir rehearsal room was not in disarray. It took a lot of tables and chairs to set up for the festival on Saturday, and although the breakdown volunteers were responsible for getting things from the parking lot back into the church, they were not responsible for arranging the rooms the way they had been before the event.

Marcus unlocked the door and turned on the light. *Wow!* He thought, *the rooms looks great.* It made him wonder if the volunteer who brought the chairs back to the room was a member of the choir. He put his music bag on the desk, and took out his Laptop. It wasn't hard to get to because the middle zipper sections on the bag had been broken for quite some time, and the outside latch was missing. He clicked on the Mouse, and hit a button or two which brought the computer to life. Next, he removed a few folders from his carrying bag. They held the sheet music he was going to use, and next he checked his cellphone for the time. He always arrived half an hour before service started; mainly to align his spirit and thoughts for the day. He also wanted to be available just in case Pastor Hastings popped in with a special request.

Darla was trying her best to hurry her mother along. She seemed just as excited about giving Brother Stillwater the dessert package as she was about seeing her friends. Casandra did a mental check of her appearance, and turned the doorknob to the choir room. She eased the door open to take a quick gander inside. *He was there.* Marcus was headed toward the piano when he heard the door open. Darla pushed past her mother saying joyfully, "He's in here mommy. Mr. Marcus is here." Marcus laid some sheet music on the piano, and turned to face Casandra and her daughter.

"Well, what do we have here?" Darla handed him the wrapped goodies. "We wanted you to have some of these delicious desserts from yesterday's festival since you helped me to win them, and mommy said I couldn't cut the cake until this morning so you could get the first slice." Immediately Marcus' eyes met Casandra's with a pleasant smile, and a raised eyebrow. She wished Darla had not phrased her announcement in those particular words. Casandra was a bit taken-back with his next statement. "Well, I'm honored by such thoughtful consideration", he said. His eyes never moved from their gaze on Casandra's face.

Just when she opened her mouth to defend herself about how her daughter phrased the cake cutting *event,* Darla rushed back to her asking if she could go find her friends. Casandra barely nodded her head, and Darla was out the door in a flash. Casandra stood there dumbfounded. She knew Marcus said something to her, but for some reason it sounded distant and muffled. "Excuse me. I had my attention on my daughter dashing out the door.

Did you say something?"

Marcus cleared his throat, and with a slight smirk on his face said, "I was complimenting you on how nice you and your daughter look today." Now, she was embarrassed beyond measure. She hoped he didn't think she was fishing for a repeated compliment. "Oh, I'm sorry. I mean thank you very much that is …I meant, thank you for me and my daughter." Casandra chided herself for rambling on. *Why do I always do that when I'm around him?*

"Say, we have a little while before service begins, have a seat, or do you have to catch up with your daughter?" Casandra knew if she refused to stay she would only be running away again. Marcus walked over to sit at the piano. God answered his prayer. She stay. Now if he could only think of something to justify his request, and remove the tension he sensed building between their silences. He had to think of something quickly before she changed her mind.

"Thank you again for the cake and brownies. I have a terrible sweet tooth. I'll try not to eat up everything before I leave church." He offered a warming smile as he moved his fingers lightly across the piano keys. "As a matter of fact, he said, I'm a real *snack-a-holic*. I have to make myself eat a decent meal." Before she could restrain from saying what her mind was thinking it popped out. "Oh, really? A person wouldn't guess that about you, because your physique is so, I mean your body is so built." *Oh my God! I can't believe I just said that!* Marcus realized Casandra was quite mortified with her pronouncement, and quickly diverted the subject.

"Thanks for sharing the booth with me yesterday. I enjoyed working with you." "Well, she said, (trying to shrug it off) I guess that's just the way the *lots* fell" Marcus stopped tickling the piano keys. He looked directly at Casandra and said, "Then I consider myself lucky, because they *fell* in my favor."

———

Lucinda saw Darla coming out of the restroom with two of her friends. She complimented the threesome on their look-a-like outfits, and asked Darla the where-a-bouts of her mother. The nine-year old said she wasn't sure where her mother was at the moment, but she left her in the choir room with Mr. Marcus. She told Lucinda she could try looking there, and then she trotted off with her friends.

Whoa! That's something I didn't expect to hear. Lucinda stood there for a minute contemplating her next move. She surely wasn't going to extend her search towards the choir room. She wondered if anything more than a casual 'hello' was brewing between the two since yesterday's festival, and she tried not to let her jealousy emerge.

Not wanting to take the chance of being seen in the hallway by her friend (should she suddenly emerge from the choir room), Lucinda darted into the sanctuary and took a seat on the pew where the two of them usually sat.

Chapter 13

Marcus felt as if he had in some way reprieved himself from whatever caused Casandra to cool off toward him yesterday. His mind wandered for just a second or two. The solid color A-line dress she had on was very flattering. She had on a triple strand of multicolor pearls that picked up the warm hue of her fall colored dress. He wanted to compliment her again, but knew that would have been too much of a *come-on*. He ended up asking her about joining the choir. He knew she probably would say no, but he just wanted to get the conversation going again.

Casandra's eyes floated toward the clock on the wall. She was sure choir members would be coming in soon, and she didn't want to be seen alone with him. She told Marcus she'd better leave because she didn't want to hold him up from his duties. He really wanted her to stay, but she was right. He should have been practicing. It was almost 10:45, and he knew the choir members would be gathering for prayer. Casandra stood up, and Marcus moved from behind the piano to walk her to the door. He was thinking hard at how to get a chance to see her again outside of a church function without it being a date-*date*. *Think,* he told himself, *think.*

Reaching ahead of her to open the door something came to mind. "Say, I'm going to the library this afternoon to do my reading session with the kids; if it's time for Darla to return her books I'd really like it if y'all would drop in." Casandra didn't know what to say. It *was* time for her daughter to return the books. "It's not until three o'clock he continued, which will give you enough time to relax a bit at home before you come out again. I remember the last time I ran into you—that is to you and Darla, you were having a 'back-pack' lunch. I think that was really sweet." He paused a second then he said. "I'll tell you what. If you come today you won't have to worry about lunch, because it will be on me."

Marcus was nervous as he could be. *Did he just ask Casandra out for a date?* "That's the least I could do seeing that Darla already brought me dessert." He flashed a warming (half pleading) smile at her, and Casandra said, "Yes." "Great! It's a date…I mean, I'll meet you at the library if I can."

———

Lucinda sat in the sanctuary waiting for her friend. As curious as Lucinda was about the information she had just gotten from Darla, she decided not to question Casandra about it. Her thoughts ran back to the day before when her inquisitiveness landed her in an awkward situation.

Casandra eased the door open to where Darla's 'Children's Church' was being held. She didn't want to say anything to her, she just wanted to be sure she had gotten to class with her friends, and they had not been side tracked.

After a *peek-see* she used the Lady's room before going in to the service. It wasn't a dire need to use the facilities at the moment, but once she got in the worship service she didn't like having to leave out—especially now since a certain pair of eyes might be following her. She lingered a minute or two at the mirror checking her make up (though she wore very little), and straightening a few strains of hair that had worked their way loose from her bun. Casandra reflected on Marcus' slight flirtation with her, and butterfly's fluttered in her stomach. She never thought about Christian men as being romantic. Marcus' comments were stirring, but tasteful. Some men didn't know how to flirt without being vulgar. But, Brother Stillwater's flirting left her feeling captivated—not used!

Casandra stood inside the doors of the sanctuary scanning the congregation for Lucinda. The slight touch on her arm gave her a *start,* and she looked to her right to see Antoinette and her family sitting in the pew near the back of the sanctuary. She greeted her sister and brother-in-law in a soft whisper, and waved at BJ who was desperately trying to break free from his father's grip, and run to her.

The choir was leading the congregation in a Praise song, so his calling out "*Aunti Sandwa*" was somewhat muffled. She put her index finger to her lips, and gave him a pleasant *'shush'* then threw him a big *hand-kiss*.

Lucinda was anxiously waiting for Casandra, and looked toward the back of the sanctuary every time she heard the slight bump of its double doors fall back into place. She was very curious about her friend being in the choir room (alone) she presumed with the church's musician, but had to restrain herself from asking Casandra about it. Her uncontained tongue placed her and her friend in an uneasy position just the day before, and she didn't want that to happen again. Besides, too many questions might disclose her own secret feelings about the handsome church musician.

Casandra approached the pew where Lucinda was seated, and excused herself as she maneuvered passed the elderly couple sitting at the end of the row. *Why was she held up so many times today?* On any other Sunday she would have already been seated, but the few minutes extra delivering the plate, then going to the choir room, the ladies' room, and stopping to speak with her family caused her to get to her seat later than usual.

She could feel several pairs of eyes on her; including those of Brother Marcus Stillwater. Casandra sat down next to Lucinda who took a quick peek at her watch. The *'Expeditor'* had just finished the 'Call to Worship' address, and took her seat. She felt a nudge on her arm. The person on the other side of her handed her the bulletin program for the morning's order of service. Lucinda whispered that she saw Darla and her friends in the hallway. She said the threesome looked so cute in their look-a-like outfits, but she didn't mention anything else.

Casandra tried to focus and reel her thoughts into the service. She was more aware than ever that Marcus glanced her way more than once. What made matters worse was that she looked his way several times too. But, she wasn't trying to catch his eye. As a matter of fact she was hoping to do the opposite. She didn't want people to follow his gaze which he directed straight towards her. However, if no one else noticed–a certain couple did, and so did Lucinda. Casandra sang along with the congregation to the seasonal hymn 'Yield Not to Temptation' which was printed on the bulletin.

Hearing her own melodious voice caused her mind to wander back to Marcus when he asked her about joining the choir. *Lord,* she thought, *why am I fooling myself? Why am I afraid of a real relationship? I'm not only alone…I'm lonely. What's wrong with me? Why am I always putting on a false face of happiness for everyone when inside I'm hurting? I'm starving for someone to care for me, and no amount of bright colored clothing and jewelry can mend this façaded heart. Please God, I want to yield to Your counsel when it comes to matters of my heart. Bring me back to life again, and stop the leaves from falling.*

Chapter 14

Marcus chided himself for staring at Casandra, because a couple of times when his eyes met hers he hoped no one noticed, but there were at least three people who did for sure. They were Deacon Anthony Campbell and his wife Belinda, and Lucinda Brown. Lucinda could sense how nervous her friend was already, so she refrained from inquiring about the information she heard from Darla. Casandra was so nervous she looked as if she could run out of the church service at any moment.

Just to ease her tension Lucinda leaned over to her left and bumped Casandra's right shoulder with hers. "Smile San. God loves you." Casandra realized her tenseness must have been showing on her face. She relaxed, took in a deep breath, and forced a smile for her friend.

When the service ended before leaving her pew Casandra looked back to where her sister was sitting with her family. She wanted to see if Darla was there. Sometimes rather than nudging her way to the front of the sanctuary where her mother was sitting; after Children's Church ended Darla would sit in the back with her Aunti. *Yes.* Darla was there.

When service ended Casandra inched her way out of the pew hoping for a way to avoid the following Lucinda, and the searching eyes of the church's musician. Lucinda was right on her heels. Casandra greeted her sister and brother-in-law again, patted BJ on his head, and collected Darla. She wanted to keep on moving, but Darla wanted her mother to take a picture of her and her two friends. She begged for her mother to wait while she went to get them. Lucinda, who was typically very talkative remained unusually quiet, so Casandra filled in the silence with comments about the wonderful church service they just had. Lucinda said it was nice, and kept her other feelings to herself.

After the *photo shoot* Casandra moved quickly to the back exit doors. She didn't want to linger around chancing an encounter with Brother Marcus, and risking an onslaught of question from Lucinda, so she briskly moved toward the exit doors waving to Lucinda over her shoulder that she was in a hurry, and she would call her later.

Lucinda waved back, but was still a bit miffed that she didn't get to ask any questions about the information she got from Darla.

———

Marcus didn't know why he was trying so hard to rush Casandra into a friendlier relationship with him. *What was the hurry?* He knew his invitation today was a bold move on his part, but at least she didn't say 'No'. For a long time he had been wanting to know Casandra in a more personal way, but that didn't mean she felt the same way about him. *What if she already has a boyfriend? Just because I've never seen her with anyone here at the church doesn't mean she's not in a relationship with someone else. Nah! If that was true, she would not have said 'yes' to meeting me at the library. She's not that type of person. I may not know her very well, but I'm sure she has better integrity than that.*

It was already one-thirty, and Marcus had not yet decided what he was going to read to the children. With all of his own preparation he remembered the one thing he failed to do—pray. He realized he put so much effort into planning what he wanted he never stopped to ask God what His plans were for him. Marcus remembered the

Bible verse that said, "Many are the plans in a man's heart, but it is God's purpose that will prevail."

He began to pray that his plans were God's plans for him too.

———

As soon as they got home Casandra told her daughter to change her clothes, and gather her books that were to be returned to the library. She then retreated to her bedroom to change into something more casual. It still was Sunday, so she didn't want to wear '*every day*' casual, but wanted to wear something that complimented her hairstyle, make-up, and the jewelry she was wearing.

Casandra tried her best to avoid going into the kitchen. The pre-cut lemon cake and brownies were beckoning her to come their way. *Maybe just a small slice.* She heard a slight grumble in her stomach. "No, she said aloud. You're not hungry!" But she really was, because she had not eaten anything substantial before going to church. Just then Darla tapped on her door. "Mommy. I've changed my clothes, and my library books are on the coffee table. Can I have a slice of cake now?

Casandra was thinking, *Poor Darla. It's been since yesterday, and she hasn't tasted the cake she won.* She couldn't deny her daughter having a piece of cake just because she was trying to avoid her own temptations. Casandra cut a piece of cake and put it on a saucer for Darla. She set a glass of milk beside it. "Umm mommy. This cake taste *really* good. Aren't you going to have some?" She hadn't told her daughter that they were going to have lunch with Brother Stillwater after their visit to the library. "No, she said. I might just wait until after lunch, or dinner." Darla wanted to know if lunch was going to be right away, because if it wasn't, she wanted to know if she could have a brownie too. Casandra cautioned her daughter about her 'sweet tooth', but who was she to talk. She laid a brownie square on Darla's saucer.

It was half past one o'clock, and she was to meet Marcus at the library around three. She knew the sweets wouldn't hold Darla for long, and she didn't want to share with her that they were going to a late Sunday lunch with the church's musician. Her thoughts were roaming back and forth. They were all over the place. Should she go to the library or not? Casandra's stomach gave a slight rumble for the second time. *Maybe a small slice of cake would halt the hunger pain creeping upon me.* She got a saucer from the cabinet, and sat at the table. She cut a medium size slice of cake and placed it on the small plate.

She was thinking—*one slice won't hurt, and I might as well see what the brownies taste like.*

Darla finished her snack, and put her glass and saucer in the sink. She asked if it would be alright if she called her friends and told them she was going to the library today. She asked her mother if she would texted her the pictures of her and her friends, and after that she wanted to play video games on her phone until it was time to go. Darla skidded off to her room, and closed the door.

Casandra sat at the table letting her thoughts run ramped. Seemingly from out of nowhere came a sudden surge of loneliness. She got up, and brewed a single cup of coffee, then sat back down and sliced another piece of cake. She reached in the container and took another brownie. Lost in a downward churn of self-pity Casandra looked at the now diminishing cake and brownie container set before her.

Why am I doing this to myself? Stop it! Stop it! Enough is enough!

She lowered her face into her hands and

began to weep—softly at first, and then she began sobbing. She made a mad dash to her bedroom; hopefully before her daughter could hear her, and the sweltering sobs that were mounting from within. Casandra wasn't sure how much time had passed. She tried her best to pull herself together. She heard a small knock on her door. It was Darla wanting to know when they were going to the library. She told her daughter something had come up that interrupted her plans. She would fix lunch soon, and they could drop her books in the library drop-box on her way to school on Monday.

Casandra knew there was no way she was going to keep her meeting with Brother Stillwater now—not with puffy red eyes, and a nose that looked the same. She hated that she let fear get the best of her. And now, she just hoped she didn't get a phone call from Marcus Stillwater.

Lucy Heath

Chapter 15

Casandra moved slowly in the task of preparing the late afternoon meal for her and Darla. The ringtone on her cell startled her. Her heart began to palpitate; thumping against her chest. She glanced at the clock in the microwave oven. It read 3:20pm. She curiously moved towards the table where she left her phone. It rang a second time. Her palms began to sweat. Casandra was almost shaking. She just knew it had to be Brother Stillwater! She didn't want to look at the phone, but she had to stop it from ringing. If it was Marcus, how could she talk to him? What excuse could she give him for not showing up? Quickly consoling herself she said. "After-all, it wasn't a date-*date*." True–it wasn't a date, and she didn't *really* promise. *Wait! Does he have my number?*

She told herself it was more like...like an agreement to meet him, *if* she could. But, she knew that wasn't the truth either. Another ring pierced the silence of her musing. She decided not to answer it. Two more rings, and it would automatically go to her voicemail. Just then Darla came sailing out of her bedroom. "Mommy, your cellphone is ringing."

Casandra had to answer it now. If it was Marcus, she couldn't let Darla hear his voice leaving her a message. She took a deep breath, and reached for the phone. With one eye closed she peeped at the lit up screen. The name read— BROWN LUCINDA. Casandra quickly grabbed the phone, and pushed the green talk button. *Although, she really didn't want to talk with her either.*

Marcus tried to focus on reading to the kids, but every time someone passed the opening to the reading room his attention was diverted. Still, he read through the story taking time to give a different voice to each of the characters. He got joy in seeing how the children's eyes lit up and sparkled with each of the story's personalities.

When the kids were that interested in the story, it made it easier for him at the end of it for the question and answer time to go smoothly. Parents were always appreciative when their child retold the story to them on the way home. Most of the parents hung around to see how interested their child was in the story, and would surprise them by checking the book out of the library, or purchasing it, if it was for sale.

Sometimes he read books that were library stock, and other times he would bring a book he had published, or read a short story he had written.

Marcus took his time gathering his things together after the session. He still was hoping that Casandra and her daughter were just running a little late, but that hope soon began to fade. The drive home seemed longer than ever before. *Had he taken a wrong turn? Nah! I couldn't have,* he thought.

———

"Hello. Hello." A voice came from the receiver. "Is anybody there?" Casandra shook herself realizing that she had swiped the screen, but hadn't said anything. "Oh. Hi Lu. Sorry I got distracted." "Are you home, or are you still out?" Casandra told her friend she was at home, but wanted to know why she was asking her about being out. Lucinda reminded her that she was in such a hurry when she left church; she thought she might have had an appointment to *meet* someone.

Casandra could sense that Lucinda was fishing for information just from the way she phrased her words, but what could she tell her—that she had a date but was too much of a *chicken* to keep it? Lucinda was her friend–as a matter of fact, her closet friend. She just wasn't sure how much of her private life she wanted to share with her. Casandra responded by saying she thought she had somewhere to be, but she changed her mind and decided to wait until tomorrow.

"*Soo* then, Lucinda said creeping up on her next question, you're sure you and Brother Stillwater weren't going to keep a secret rendezvous?" Casandra gasped! *What did Lucinda know? Did she talk with Marcus after she left church?* She felt her dander raise. *How dare her meddle in my private affairs!* Instead she said (very weakly) "What makes you say a thing like that?" "Oh come on San. As much eye contact that was going on between you two in Church I knew something had to be going on!"

Casandra still didn't know what to say. Lucinda continued to talk. "Look San, we've been friends for—at least five years now. You're my best friend. I know you pretty good by now, and it's alright." "What's alright?" "San, it's alright to like somebody. Let down your guard. The past is past! Brother Marcus is a good Christian man. He's safe. He won't hurt you. What are you afraid of?"

Lucinda really wanted to say how much she adored Marcus, but she knew she wasn't the right one for him. As much as she wanted to be…he never gave her a second glance.

———

Marcus paced back and forth across the kitchen floor. He was truly distraught. *What happened? Where did I mess up?* He stopped pacing, and sat for a minute or two, and then got up. He knew he was becoming emotional. He walked through the living room, and circled back around to the kitchen. In the midst of his anxiety his stomach gave a small rumble. Shortly after, another one followed—even louder. His emotions saddened even more remembering; not only had Casandra not come to the story hour with her daughter, but that meant he was unable to keep their lunch outing too.

Marcus grabbed a bottle water from the fridge, and sat at the kitchen table. He was hungry, but he didn't want to eat. Eating now would only remind him of how alone he was. He figured maybe since he was hurting he might as well make his stomach suffer too. Marcus took his phone from his back pants pocket, and laid it on the table. He needed to be consoled by listening to some music.

Yes, some easy jazz. No. Maybe I'll call my Dad. But what could I tell him? How would I start my conversation? *This is crazy!* He thought. *I'm a thirty-two year old man, and I haven't come to my dad recently with any of my problems. It has to be something deeper than—I don't know what to do because a girl stood me up for a date.*

Marcus' stomach gave a twang of slight pain. He decided that one type of suffering was enough, and started to fix something to eat, but he didn't want to prepare anything that would remind him of the restaurant he was going to take Casandra, and Darla to—even if it was just one of those pancake house places.

He decided to fix one of his favorite easy things to make–a grilled cheese sandwich. Yelp! That would do the trick. Marcus still hadn't verbally prayed about the relationship he desired to have with Casandra, so that put a check in his spirit when a lot of negative emotions started pouring into his mind.

He decided to eat his grilled cheese sandwich, and call his dad later. Actually—he was still being nudged to pray. He slowly moved to the living room sofa, and quieted himself before the Lord. Marcus prayed that his will was God's Will for him, and then he sensed a Bible scripture in his thinking that said it aloud.

"For I know the thoughts that I think towards you, says the Lord, thoughts of peace, and not of evil, to give you an *expected* end. Then shall you call upon me, and you shall go and pray unto me, and I will harken unto you and you shall seek me, and find me when you shall search for me with all your heart." [Jeramiah 29:11-13]

Marcus knew the scripture well, but he always related it to being successful in business, or having success in ministry. He never thought it could directly relate to him finding a wife. "Wow", he thought! *Is God telling me to search Him with all my heart? I know I try to be the best Christian man I can, but I never considered that more of my heart wanted other things than it wanted to be closer to God.*

After he finished praying Marcus felt led to call Deacon Campbell instead of him dad. He knew some time had passed since he and his dad had a chat, and when he called him he wanted something less stressful to talk about.

Chapter 16

Casandra called Lucinda to say she was right. She told her about the events of the day, and said she now felt embarrassed, and too ashamed to call Brother Stillwater to apologize. She admitted she *could* be interested in Brother Marcus, but refused to say any more than that–remembering that Lucinda once told her that she had been attracted to him too. Since Casandra wasn't altogether sure where her friend was with those feelings she decided to tread softly with her comments.

Lucinda reminded Casandra that the 'Singles' meeting was Wednesday night, and strongly suggested that she didn't back out of going. She told her it would make it much harder to face up to her fears the next time she saw Brother Stillwater; especially now with two hurdles to overcome.

Of course Lucinda was right. They talked for a few minutes more, and Casandra wanted to know what she should do. She knew Marcus would be at the meeting, and she just couldn't sit across from him looking, and feeling dreadfully ashamed.

That's when Lucinda came up with a good idea. She suggested that she could write him a personal note apologizing in her own personal way. She could write it on one of those 'Thank You' note cards expressing he regret—saying that something unexpected came up at the last minute(not saying it was her fears), and if he would ask her again; she would be sure that nothing got in the way.

Casandra loved the idea. The note would be in her own handwriting (which was very personable), and she would make sure she was either sitting across from him, or at least close enough to him to pass the note—Lucinda could see to that. After that was settled the friends said goodbye. Casandra's nervousness began to fade away, and a slight smile came upon her face. She actually felt a sense of relief in her heart.

It never entered her mind that on Wednesday evening—in her forthwith venture, she was actually going to ask Marcus out on a date.

It was getting later in the evening, and Casandra was feeling a strong urge to eat some sweets. Sunday dinner was usually a couple of hours earlier than her regular weekday dinner time because of her job, and having to pick Darla up from Aftercare. She knew there were healthier snacks in the cabinet and fridge, but she kept being drawn to the remaining brownies and the large chunk of lemon cake left from Saturday's Fall Festival. *Maybe just a sliver,* she thought, but she knew herself better than that. Once her taste buds got ahold of sweets; they didn't want to let go. Darla was more apt to want brownies in her school lunch rather than cake—so cake it would be.

Casandra stood between the living room and the kitchen fighting her desire to devour the rest of the lemon cake. She wished she had something to do to take her mind off of eating. She knew she wasn't one for following diet plans, or those well-known 'weight lost' programs, but she had to do something! She had to stop turning to food as a solace for every problem. *Maybe if I had a hobby, or some sort of craft that could keep my mind occupied in my free time.* She chided herself saying–*how can I break the cycle when I'm only listening to that one negative voice that's constantly in my ear saying–*Eat, eat, eating something will help!

The ring of her cellphone caused her to jump, and she retrieved it from her pocket.

"Hey Sis, didn't have a chance to call you after church. Things got really busy once I got home. What' sup?" Casandra was grateful for the timely interruption. *Thank God,* she thought. She was glad it was Antoinette. She felt like asking advice, and she could trust her sister with her feelings. She was not just her sister; she was her *'bestie'.* Her sister's phone call was right on time, and an answer to her prayer. Antoinette called to say she had prepared a huge Sunday dinner, and she was on her way over with enough food for everyone. She said she wanted to call first to be sure they had not already eaten. Casandra thanked God she was saved from delving into the sweets, and she would had a listening ear to boot!

―――――

Marcus shared a little of his quandary with Deacon Campbell, and the Deacon asked if he would mind if he put them on speakerphone so his wife could listen in. Marcus was a little apprehensive, but said yes. The Deacon said he probably could be helpful in advising him from a man's point of view, but when it came to a woman's mind—he'd been married for thirty years and still couldn't figure it out. In the background

Marcus heard Sister Campbell retort—"and you never will!" All three of them got a good laugh out of that.

The husband and wife team agreed Marcus was on the right tract, and moving in the right direction. Sister Campbell said she knew some of Casandra's background concerning her divorce, but was not at liberty to share any particulars; although she did say Marcus was the only man she had ever seen Sister Russell talk with. That was encouraging to Marcus. Deacon Campbell warned him that every woman was different, and not to consolidate what he thought he knew about women into one package—supposing that was what Casandra was like, because it wouldn't work. The couple shared some words of encouragement, and ended the call with a short prayer.

Marcus was glad he called the Campbell's. He thought about the last statement Deacon Campbell made, and knew he was on the right track because that's what drew him to Casandra in the first place. She wasn't loud and flashy like some of the other single lady's. It was her reserve mannerism, and the discreet way her inner beauty shown through that got his attention. Now he knew how he wanted to pray. He went to his bedroom, and sat in the chair.

"Father pour Your horn of oil upon me as a man of God, that I will not be tempted by the lust of the flesh. Help me to know Casandra's heart, and to be drawn to the glory You placed in her, Amen."

———

Casandra took her lunch break an hour later than she usually did because she was sure the break room would not be crowded. She wasn't antisocial. She just wanted a little more privacy to jot down some thoughts of what she wanted to write to Brother Marcus. She sat for a few minutes in quiet solitude, and a thought came to her. It had nothing to do with the note, but she wondered; *why do people always say, it's better to have loved and lost than never to have loved at all?* 'It's not better, she thought. *It hurts like crazy! And, most of the time people who say that, still have someone who loves them.*

Before she realized it her lunch hour had dwindled away, and she had not written one word. "Well, she sighed aloud, at least I only have three more hours until I'm off work."

Casandra drove up to a parking spot close to the school, and went in to pick up Darla. Mr.

Williams greeted her in his usual friendly manner, and reported that Darla had made tremendous progress over the past couple of months. He said he only had to spot-check her work every now and then; otherwise she was doing her math assignments without his assistance. As they were leaving out he said how much he enjoyed the church festival. Casandra thanked him for his financial support, and said she was glad he was able to come.

On Wednesday Casandra prepared one of her quick *go-to* meals—spaghetti with meat sauce. She made a chef salad, and baked the prepared frozen garlic bread in the oven. After dinner she cleared the table, and Darla dashed to her room to finish the couple pages of reading she had to do for English. *Was it Wednesday night already? What happened to Tuesday?* Casandra breathed in some deep breaths and went to her bedroom. It was only five-thirty, and this was the second time she changed her mind about what she was going to wear.

She brushed her teeth, then came back and sat on the side of the bed, and reached for her purse. She removed the small envelope that held the note she had written to Marcus Stillwater. She wanted to be sure her words were honest, but not misunderstood. She had written the note so many times over the last couple of days she almost forgot what she ended up saying–besides that, she wanted to check once again for any spelling errors.

Casandra opened the note, and began to read.

Brother Marcus,

I apologize for letting something sidetrack me from keeping our engagement on Sunday. However, if you will ask me again, I will be sure that nothing gets in the way,

Cordially,

Casandra Russell

She knew this was the craziest thing she had ever done—well *almost the craziest thing* she had ever done in her life, but she felt good about it.

Chapter 17

Casandra knew Lucinda didn't mind helping her out, but the more she thought about it the more she was having second thoughts about her friend's involvement. After all it wasn't like they were high school teenagers. They were adults. The other matter was that she didn't want to cause any embarrassment to Brother Marcus. She had to think about how he would feel having Lucinda pass him a note knowing that it might be a personal message in it from her. He might even think that Lucinda knew what was in the note. No, that was not going to work! She wasn't about to start off a more involved relationship with a man by embarrassing the very person she was apologizing to.

Lucinda was waiting for Casandra near the entrance of the Fellowship Hall where the 'Singles' held their meetings. She could see the excitement on Lucinda's face. Casandra now regretted she shared the whole matter with her. She cautiously approached Lucinda, and before she lost her nerve, she rushed the words out of her mouth. "Lu, thanks for all of your help, but I decided to go about this in a different way." The enthusiasm immediately dwindled from Lucinda's face, and was replaced by a look of disappointment, so Casandra quickly told her friend that she still was going to use her idea with the note, but go about getting it to Marcus in a different way. With that, she could see the disappointment lift from Lucinda's face–though not completely because she knew how much her friend liked to be in the forefront of things.

Casandra knew that Brother Stillwater would be attending the 'Singles' meeting when the 'Praise and Worship' portion of the service ended. A new idea popped into her head. She asked her friend to save a seat for her in the meeting while she made sure Darla was settled in her youth meeting. She also said she would probably stop by the ladies room before coming in.

Lucinda opened the doors to the Fellowship Hall, and looked back over her shoulder to say, "Don't worry San. You look fine." Casandra waved her friend off, and turned to go down the hall. When she was sure Lucinda was in the soon to begin meeting, she ducked in the doors to the sanctuary.

This was such a crazy, bold move on her part, and her hands were shaking. She froze when just inside the door Brother Stillwater's head turned in her direction, and his eyes locked with her. She wanted to do a U-turn, and escape back out the door, but she knew if she did that she would either have to dismiss her sudden new plan, or grab up Darla, and go home.

Deacon Campbell was in the sanctuary sitting on the first row. Casandra assumed Sister Campbell was already in the Fellowship Hall preparing for the meeting, and any early arrivers. Her eyes darted back and forth scanning the audience looking for open seating. Wednesday night Bible study drew a smaller crowd than the regular Sunday morning services, and was even slimmer due to the fact that other classes and meeting were being held nearly, or close to the same time.

Casandra didn't want to sit too far near the front of the church because she wasn't staying for Bible Study—yet she didn't want to be so far in the rear that she would have to pass a lot of people to get her note to Marcus. She was not sure where

she should sit. *Maybe this wasn't such a good idea.*
Realizing she was standing in the middle of the
aisle, she scurried to sit in the pew on the left side
of the sanctuary facing where the band was.

Marcus tried to concentrate on playing the
worship songs, but was embarrassed when he
struck a few wrong cords. It probably went
unnoticed by the congregation, but Pastor Hastings
(who knew his expertise as a musician) raised her
head from the open Bible on her lap, and looked
his way. Although she didn't show any sort of real
concern he was embarrassed just the same.

The last worship song was at its ending
stanza, and Marcus nodded for the other musicians
to slow the tempo. When Pastor Hastings stood he
nodded again, and the band lowered the volume of
their playing, leaving a soft trail of melodious notes
whispering in the air.

Casandra smiled to herself taking in the
caring nurture of Brother Stillwater's playing. She
must have mused on it a few moments longer than
intended, because the movement of a person in the
pew ahead of her shifted her focus back to the
situation at hand. How was she to get the note to
Marcus? She knew he was going to leave the band
area shortly to attend the 'Singles' meeting. On

Sundays when service was over, he usually left through the door located on the pulpit level next to the band area.

Deacon Campbell stood, and eased his way from the pew to exit the sanctuary. Casandra knew he was leaving to join his wife in leading the meeting. She noticed several others tipping out softly realizing they must have come to be in on the Praise and Worship part of Bible study before they went to their alternative meetings.

Casandra turned her focus to the pulpit area, and Marcus was looking directly at her. He was still seated at the organ playing softly. Her thought was to leave out while other movement was going on, but just as soon as she started to move Pastor Hastings approached the podium and began an opening prayer. All movement ceased, with heads bowed in quiet reverence.

Sister Belinda Campbell opened the 'Singles' meeting with prayer, and asked that one of the attendees read a Bible scripture of their choice. Renita Scott volunteered, and read <u>Psalms 34:8 – "O taste and see that the Lord is good: blessed is the man that</u>

trust in Him."

Lucinda turned her eyes towards the double doors every time they opened. *Where is Casandra? Did she chicken-out?* She hoped her friend had not gone home. Deacon Anthony Campbell trotted through the doors apologizing for being late—as he did for most meetings; unless his wife attended Praise and Worship, and then she was the one who came in apologizing.

Lucinda began to worry when Brother Stillwater came through the doors and took a seat at one of the tables. He gave an open greeting to the group, and Sister Campbell began to read the agenda for the evening.

Finally Casandra came in, and took a seat next to Lucinda. She leaned into Casandra's arm, but with her hand in her lap Casandra signaled moving her index finger back and forth—not now. Lucinda kept darting her eyes toward Casandra trying to get her attention. She gave her friend a slight smile, but Lucinda couldn't draw anything from it. She finally gave up, not wanting to draw attention to them and away from the meeting. Casandra knew her friend felt slighted by not being able to be in control of the immediate situation, but that was how it had to be for now.

Lucinda spent the whole evening trying to read any expressions that were passed between Marcus, and Casandra, but there were none. Everything seemed to going on as usual. *'Bummer'*, she thought. *San probably chickened out!*

The Campbell's were suggesting a Christmas gathering and secret gift exchange for the holiday, and wanted to know what the group thought about it. They still had a little over six weeks to plan for the affair, and get it in the announcements. Next, they wanted to know by a show of hands how many of the group would be in town should they decide to go forward with the event, and how many had already made plans to be with family, or to be out of town for Christmas. The Campbell's asked one member of the group to draw up a list people who were going to be out of town. By a show of hands, it looked like most of them were staying in Blackburn.

Lucinda was among the few who had already made plans to be out of town.

A quick connection of eye contact happened between Marcus and Casandra, when they realized that they both were going to be in town for the holiday. At that moment Lucinda was a bit sorry she had already made plans to travel. Her mom and dad were expecting her this year for Christmas, because she had not come to visit them last year. *'Man,* she thought! *I just know I'm going to miss out on something interesting between Casandra and Marcus.* She felt a sudden twinge of jealously.

———

Marcus drove home trying to remain calm. The unread note seemed to be burning a hole in his pant pocket. He thought about how he would usually leave the musician's area through the side door, but having seen Casandra he thought he could make another attempt to speak with her. He had almost reached her when the sanctuary doors closed behind her. A feeling of dismay swooped over him, but disappeared immediately when he stepped in the hallway and saw her waiting—with any luck, she was waiting for him. A sliver of hope sprang up in his heart.

Casandra voiced a quick hello, and passed him the note. She asked him not to read it until after the meeting. He had noticed a shy, inocent blush come across her face, so maybe the note wasn't a disheartening one.

Marcus placed his music attachè case on the

kitchen counter, and went directly to the bedroom. He didn't know what was written in the note, he just supposed whatever it was it would be better reading it in the confines of his bedroom—he felt safe there. He tossed his jacket across the chair, felt for the note in his pants pocket, and sat on the edge of the bed.

'*Uhm*', he thought admiring his name on the outside of the envelope– '*beautiful handwriting*'. His inner voice interrupted his musing saying–*Are you just going to sit there smiling at her handwriting, or are you going to open the note?* Marcus' hands trembled as he fished the folded note from its holder.

Brother Marcus,

I apologize for letting something sidetrack me from keeping our engagement on Sunday. However, if you will ask me again, I will be sure that nothing gets in the way.

Cordially,

Casandra Russell

Marcus read the note several times. The words…ask me again, lifted off the page, and hung in his mind. He was trying to go through his usual preparations for retiring for the evening—

thanking God for the goodness of the day, and for directing his path in all things, but tonight he laid down with additional hope in his heart, and a little something tucked under his pillow.

Chapter 18

Casandra told her sister all that had transpired between her and Marcus. Antoinette was elated. It had been six years since her sister's divorce from Marvin, and except for that short interlude with Raymond (who turned out to be quit deceptive) no other men had been in her life, nor Darla's.

Antoinette wanted to know if Casandra thought Marcus would call her before Sunday. She told her probably not because she purposely didn't put her contact information in the note. She told her when she didn't keep the engagement at the library she was almost had a nervous breakdown when she thought Marcus was calling her, but then she remembered he didn't have her phone number. She said she didn't put it in the note either because that would have been too forward for her. Besides, she needed a few days to think about how bold she had been, and to pray she wouldn't back out.

Casandra decided to visit the library on

Saturday instead of Sunday. After her recent blunder she wasn't sure of how Sunday's would work for the library. October had slowly crossed over into the month of November, and the weather was chilly and breezy calling for the need of a light jacket, or heavy sweater. On Friday Darla brought home a list of suggested books to read for the two book reports due after Thanksgiving break, and the one other before Christmas break. The class had six weeks to complete their assignment. That was two weeks longer than they usually had, but only because the reports now required three to four written pages instead of the usual two, and because they also had the additional days out of school for the longer Thanksgiving break.

Darla loved to read, but Casandra wasn't sure which books on the list would capture and hold her daughter's interest. She meandered through the shelves with Darla, and couldn't find two of the books on the list, so she went to the front desk to inquire about them. The Liberian told her those books had already been checked out. Casandra figured those must have been the easier ones to read. It wasn't that Darla needed easier books to read; she tested a grade and a half higher in reading than her own grade level. Casandra wanted to check out a book that would hold her daughter's attention all the way through to the end. She appreciated that the teacher included some of the *'old school'* titles too.

Casandra went back to the shelves to help Darla select some books. She told her to select three books for her reports, and another for extra-curricular reading at home—basically to avoid too much phone time talking with friends, or playing games using the excuse of being bored.

That left them to choose between: 'Diary of a Wimpy Kid, by Jeff Kinney', but that was too illustrated. Heidi, by Johanna Spyri (an original classic) 'The Hunchback of Norte Dame', by Victor Hugo—hopefully the library had the children's version, and 'The Christmas Shoes', by Donna VanLiere. All of the books were a good read, but Casandra and Darla wanted a holiday story. So they also chose 'Heidi'.

Casandra checked the books due dates on her phone calendar to make sure the reports weren't due before the books had to be returned. It seemed the library extended the due back dates knowing the children would be out of school longer during the Thanksgiving break. While looking at her calendar she wondered what the date would be for the 'Singles' Christmas gathering.

The Russell family usually went to their grandparent's house for Thanksgiving, so there was no conflict there. She and Darla would go to Antoinette's for Christmas, or have Christmas dinner with the Turners—Russell's folks. This year December 25th fell on a Sunday, which meant that Christmas Eve was on a Saturday. With any luck her office would be closed that Friday, and they might even close on Thursday in order to give the employees a full three days off before the holiday.

'This is crazy!' It was getting close to the weekend, and Marcus was as nervous as a cat in a room full of rocking chairs. He thought, *'How many times have I imagined this upcoming moment in my head?* The familiar scenario became a moving picture in his mind. He would park his car in front of Casandra's apartment building, scale up the steps and knock on her door. She would be ready and waiting. He would hold the car door open for her until she was seated, and then run around to hop in the driver's seat. At the restaurant she would select something from the menu, and then allow him to

order both of their meals, and while they were waiting their conversation would flow with ease.

At least that was the way he pictured it all in his mind. So, why was he so nervous? Marcus wanted to wait until Saturday to have his car washed and detailed. That in return would free him up to go to the barber shop early Friday morning. By doing that, he wanted to accomplish two things. One, he wanted to avoid the usual early evening guys getting ready for their Friday night dates, and on Sunday he didn't want to look like he had just gotten a haircut. For some odd reason a haircut a day, or two ahead of time still made him look smooth and put together without making him look like he was trying too hard. Besides, on Sunday he knew he was going to—ask her again!

Marcus had some ideas of how he wanted their first date to be, but those ideas were still up in the air. Since he envisioned her choosing something from a menu, and him placing both of their orders with the Server. For that reason he knew a buffet style restaurant was out of the question. Besides, those restaurants were full of church patrons after their Sunday services, and he was pretty sure Casandra would shy away from that–especially on their first date. Who could tell who they might run into? And, when he thought about it he wouldn't want that for himself either.

Yes, he thought, *something a little less public, and maybe not so close to home.* Marcus knew he really meant; *not so close to their church surroundings!* With that out of the way he still had one more dilemma—how to let her know he wanted to ask her out on Sunday? Was it too soon? After all, it had only been three days since he got her note. *Should I write her a note?* Marcus knew his heart was moving faster than his head was thinking. This would take some more thought.

———

Antoinette told Casandra she was prepared to watch Darla should the *event* take place this Sunday. She said she had a little craft project she wanted to do for Thanksgiving, and she was sure her niece would want to help, and even if she got preoccupied with BJ that would still be a great help to her.

Antoinette was elated that her sister's self-confidence had surfaced. She smiled at the boldness Casandra displayed in writing the note, and thought, *she must really be drawn to Bro. Stillwater.*

Lucinda called Casandra on Friday. They hadn't been in touch since Wednesday night's 'Singles' meeting. Casandra was purposely vague with her about what was in the note to make amends for standing Brother Stillwater up on last Sunday. Lucinda was very curious, but also somewhat offended that her best friend had not shared the outcome of the ordeal with her. Casandra was aware of her friend's previous feelings toward Marcus, and still wasn't quite sure of where her feelings stood even now, so she treaded lightly around the subject saying nothing had been settled yet. Which, was not entirely a lie.

The ladies talked on for a few minutes more, and the matter seemed to have left Lucinda's mind, because she jumped on a different subject altogether. Shopping! Lucinda suggested they go shopping on Saturday for Casandra's birthday. She said Casandra should wear something new and exciting on Sunday. Casandra reminded her friend although they both were single (that unlike her) she was a divorcee with a nine year old daughter, and she had to watch her budget. She said she wasn't going to spend money she didn't have just to try and impress some man. Casandra told her if she brought anything in the way of clothing before the year was out, it would probably be something for the 'Singles' Christmas gathering.

There was a moment of silence on the other end of the line, and then pushing past a fleeting *pang*, Lucinda said, "Ca-san-dra, I'm not talking about Christmas, or trying to impress anybody. I'm talking about for your birthday. I know it's not until Monday, but it still would be nice to wear something new on Sunday…come on admit it!" With all the frazzle concerning Brother Stillwater, Casandra had completely forgotten about her own birthday. Her ear tuned back into the present phone conversation, and Lucinda was saying; "and who's talking about your budget? I want to buy my friend a new outfit for her birthday. After all, it isn't everyday a best friend of mine turns twenty-nine. Girl, I'm gonna have you twenty-nine, and looking fine!" "Wow, Casandra said, where did the years go?" "Behind you I hope" Lucinda said. Before saying goodbye the ladies decided the time and place they were going to meet at the Mall. Casandra thanked her friend again, and pushed the 'End-call' button.

Chapter 19

The coming Sunday was Holy Communion Sunday (partaking of The Lord's Supper). Brother Stillwater was not one of the pastors, or an ordained deacon, so he was not required to wear any type of official *garb,* however being the lead musician he always dressed in a suit and tie, and encouraged the other musicians to do the same. He was glad his '*asking her again*' fell on a first Sunday; that way he could wear his suit without looking like he was dressing for a special occasion.

Lucinda knew Casandra was very particular about the way she dressed. Although they were close friends, they had completely different personalities, and styles of dressing. Casandra was a little weighty, but (Lucinda had to admit) her style of dressing wasn't because of her weight. It was just that Casandra was more of a classy lady than she was. It wasn't just in the way she dressed. It was almost everything about her—her speech, her mannerisms, and her attractiveness. Casandra just didn't know it! How they ever got to be best friends she didn't know. She guessed it was a true saying: *'Opposites attract',* even in circles of friends.

Casandra often told Lucinda she wished she could be bold enough like her to approach a stranger and start up a conversation about nothing in particular. But, Lucinda thought about the times she often embarrassed herself by being too loud, and too meddlesome making herself the center of attention, and regretting it later.

The birthday shopping spree was a success. There were only a handful of shops in the Mall that sold the type of elegant clothing Lucinda wanted to buy for her friend. She wanted something that would enhance her appearance a notch upward—yet, not holler *'Look at me'.* She knew Casandra would object to the cost of the clothes, but that was the whole purpose of the shopping spree–to buy things for 'San San' she wouldn't buy for herself.

It wasn't that she was a penny-pinching miser. She had a child to think of, and Lucinda didn't. They ended with a classy two-piece red knit suit. Casandra wanted something a little more mundane, but Lucinda wouldn't hear of it. The jacket sported a double row of gold military buttons down the front, and three gold buttons at the vent of each cuff. The tapered mid-length skirt was just her style, and was an excellent fit. Lucinda added a cotton wool blend sweater with embellished metallic bling at the neckline to top off the ensemble (to wear for later), and a pair of calf high boots that had a three inch heel. Not only was the outfit a perfect birthday gift, but by mixing and matching it with other pieces it would be great for the holiday as well.

Marcus had not figured out if he needed a reason why he was going to ask Casandra out for dinner after church or not, but just in case he needed one, he had a written note of his own in his pocket. He wanted to be discrete, but he didn't want to come off as juvenile. He arrived at church early as he usually did, but sat in his car to collect his thoughts. Marcus knew he couldn't waste too much time pondering over his dilemma. Before going to the choir room he would have to check with Pastor Hastings to see if she had any additional instructions for the band.

On his way to her office he thought, *why can't I just walk up to Casandra and ask her out? It's not like people haven't see us talking with each other—after all, we did share a booth together all day at the fall festival.* Pastor Hastings had nothing to add, and said she trusted Marcus to be sensitive to the move of the Holy Spirit, and carry the service through. He left her office, and took a detour through the sanctuary to check the instruments and to do a mic check with the sound booth. Having only a short time before the praise team was to meet in the choir room, he took a short cut through the Fellowship Hall.

Walking across the corridor he heard the doors to the back entryway of the church open. He stopped in his tracks. It was Casandra and her daughter. His eyes fell on Casandra. She was stunning! Casandra looked up in surprise. She was able to emit a whisper of a *"hello"*. Marcus couldn't remember if he responded, or not. Darla ran toward him. "Hello Mr. Marcus. My mom's birthday is tomorrow, but she is wearing her new birthday outfit today. Doesn't she look beautiful?"

That did it! Casandra wanted to drop through the floor. "Darla!" The strong rebuke echoed intensely in the nearly empty corridor. Marcus released a hidden chuckle, but inwardly he agreed with Darla. He reached out, and putting his hand on her shoulder, then leaning forward speaking in a hushed tone he said, "I know you didn't intend to, but I think you embarrassed your mom a bit. And, by the way, I totally agree with you. She looks very pretty."

Marcus walked the innocent Darla the few steps back to her mother. "Good morning Casandra. You look beautiful today, as you always do." Now she really felt the warmth come to her cheeks, but managed to whisper a soft thank you. It was then that he realized he had addressed her by her first name, and not Sister Russell, or Sister Casandra as he usually did in a church setting.

Darla skipped off down the corridor leaving the two of them alone. Marcus felt a little awkward, but this was the perfect opportunity to ask her out for dinner—no note needed. He cleared his throat and said, "As a pre-birthday jester Sister Russell may I have the pleasure of taking you out to dinner today?" "Yes. I'd like that very much." Marcus sensed the low tone of voices coming down the corridor. He reached for Casandra's hand, and giving it a gentle squeeze said he would meet her after service. He moved towards the rehearsal room, but turned on his heels to say thank you. He went in and closed the door behind him. Marcus stood with his back against the door. He inhaled, then exhaled a couple of deep breaths. He couldn't believe how fast his heart was racing.

Casandra looked up to see Antoinette leaning against the wall next to the sanctuary doors. When the sisters were standing next to each other Antoinette said, "From the looks of things I guess you'll be needing a babysitter this afternoon." Casandra nodded her head yes. "By the way Sis, you do look fabulous! Happy early birthday."

The sisters entered the sanctuary, and Casandra found her usual seat near the front of the sanctuary next to Lucinda. She couldn't help but notice a few heads turning in her direction as she took her seat. Thankfully; as far as she could determine they were looks of approval. "You look *photo-shoot* perfect girl!" Lucinda commented (a little too loudly) on her friend's appearance floating her hand from head to toe. "Your hair, your makeup, your jewelry, your nails, your…your— everything is *perfect!*" Casandra leaned in. "Shhh, lower your voice. You're causing people to stare." "Girl please! They were staring at you anyway. I mean you always look good, but today—Lucinda snapped her fingers, hold back the *Paparazzi!*"

Chapter 20

After service Antoinette and Anthony took Darla home with them. That was the easy part. Casandra knew there was still the ordeal of letting Lucinda know what her plans were. She really had no choice after Lucinda suggested to take her out to dinner for her birthday, saying she looked *too* good to be going back home. Casandra knew it would be another ten minutes or so before Marcus wrapped up his usual duties after morning service, and knowing her friend's flamboyant ways she decided to share the news when they were outside of the building.

She asked Lucinda to walk to the car with her, because there was something she had to get. *Casandra knew that something was away from listening ears.* Lucinda exploded with glee. Of course she took some of the credit for the breakthrough event. Casandra put an immediate halt to Lucinda's request of wanting to know *every* detail of her and Marcus' dating relationship. Casandra said she didn't mind sharing some of her own feelings, but she wasn't about to expose any personal feelings of Brother Stillwater, or relay any private matters between the two of them. Casandra wasn't sure where that burst of boldness came from, but she was darn proud of herself for having said it!

Marcus held the passenger door open for Casandra. She was glad he drove his car to church. She knew he owned one of those SUV's. He used it the day of the church's fall festival. However, being the lady she was, and having worn a skirt that tapered down as it neared the hemline, she didn't like spreading her legs *that* wide in order to hop up into that type of vehicle. Nor did she feel comfortable hoisting her rear-end up in a man's face while trying to get into his vehicle. No. She preferred a car. It seemed much more lady-like for dating.

On the way to the selected Sea Food restaurant they mainly talked about church, and surprisingly enough their conversation was not as strained as she thought it would be. When the name *'Stillwater'* was called to be seated he stood up and she stood too. Casandra felt a wired kind of feeling in her stomach—standing to the name of 'Stillwater'. Marcus on the other hand was not sure if he was to precede the lady, or walk behind her. It had been so long since he dated, but he surmised the same gentlemanly ethics would apply here as in other situations—*Lady's first!*

He gestured a hand wave for Casandra to go ahead of him. Marcus noticed eyes inadvertently turn in their direction as the two of them trailed behind the Server. Some of the women gave a pleasant smile, and the men nodded their head to him. In the eye of a common observer it looked like a general greeting, but in the unspoken *code* of the 'Elite Gentleman', that nod gave high appraisal of the lady he was with. Marcus returned their acknowledgement with a nod of his own. He knew it was because of the *lady* in front of him, and he felt a sense of pride to be walking with her.

———

Lucinda knew it was an awful thing to do, but something came over her when she went to her car. She waited until Marcus' car turned out of the church parking lot, and then she followed it. Lucinda hated that she was jealous. She had no reason (other than rejection) to be. But, if anyone knew what rejection felt like it was Casandra. Lucinda tried to convince herself that she was miffed because Casandra—in so many words; told her it was none of her business what she and Marcus did on their date. Of course that was true, but the notion of it all made her more determined to have her way.

Did she secretly wish it was her Marcus was taking out for dinner? *This is absolutely ridiculous! What am I going to do anyway when I get there?* As much as she told herself her feelings for Marcus were over, some of them still lingered on. She wanted the best for Casandra. San deserved it. "This is ludicrous! What's wrong with me? I know Marcus doesn't have the slightest feelings for me–he never has!"

The horn from the car behind her sounded a long blast. The light had turned green, and she never even realized it. Lucinda took her foot of the brake, and zoomed forward. By now she had almost lost sight of Marcus' car, because he and Casandra were a couple of cars ahead of her, and the traffic light was still green when they passed through it. Lucinda stretched her neck trying to see past the line of cars now ahead of her.

She knew she was alone in the car, so it frightened her when she thought she heard a voice say, "*Stop this foolishness before you ruin things for your friend!*" She knew *that* voice. She had heard it in her spirit before. Lucinda clicked on her turn signal, and gradually maneuvered the car over to the left hand lane. She drove to the next intersection, and then turned the car back towards home.

The Server stopped at a table and placed two menus near the place settings. Marcus stepped in front of Casandra to slide her chair out from the table. She stood in front of the chair, and then she inched one of her legs backwards feeling for the rim of the chair. When her leg touched the chair she continued in one effortless movement (smoothing the back of her skirt) while she bent her legs, and halting momentarily as Marcus slid the chair forward beneath her. She then lowered herself to the chair in a full upright seating position keeping one leg slightly in front of the other.

Marcus took his seat across from Casandra pondering the manner in which she allowed herself to be seated. It was so feminine, so elegant. He remembered seeing things like that in the movies, or when a queen was being seated, but he never thought he would be privy to that in real life; especially not from someone he was taking on a date.

The Server returned with their soft drinks, and a basket of its special biscuits. Casandra loved those biscuits! She could have eaten the entire basket of them. However, before they were served she made a promise to herself to eat no more than two. She and Marcus had already talked about church things on their dive to the restaurant, so now their conversation didn't seem to flow as freely.

In order for it not to end up being a question and answer session Casandra remembered seeing something on YouTube about making conversation on your first date smoother. The person suggested that each of them could ask the other to share something interesting about themselves; like where they went on their last vacation, or an interesting childhood memory. Those types of questions would give your date an opportunity to talk more freely about themselves, and would help to extend the conversation time. It would also allow you to discover things about their character, and their likes and dislikes.

In just a few minutes her defensive walls came down, although not completely. She still was a little nervous. The Server returned with their meal, and Marcus said a prayer over the food. Casandra whispered, "Thank God", but she was not sanctioning the grace. She was thankful Brother Stillwater didn't reach across the table to hold hands as some people do, otherwise he would have felt icy cold hands, and nervous fingers.

Casandra became more at ease sitting with Marcus. She had eaten in his presence before, but that was casually at the church festival, and in the Fellowship Hall. Now, she was more mindful not to talk before she finished chewing her food, and to eat bite-size portions. Casandra could sense whenever Marcus' eyes were on her, and purposely tried to avoid looking directly at him. He complemented her again on her well put together look, and said how much he always enjoyed seeing her at church.

Much to her surprise he admitted wanting to talk with her on a more social level, and was pleased when he found out they were going to share a booth together at the church festival. Casandra gave a sweet smile, however her inner thought was—*Wait a minute! He knew ahead of time that we were going to share a booth together.*

When Darla asked where her mother went, Antoinette didn't feel it necessary to hide from Darla the fact that Brother Stillwater was taking her mother to dinner for her birthday. She was sure he didn't know it was Casandra's birthday, but thought it best not to make the outing seem like a pre-planned event.

Darla was pleased. She said she was glad Mr. Marcus (as she called him) asked her mom out, because she looked too beautiful to come back home, or to go to dinner with her friend Lucinda. Antoinette tried to hide her laugh as Darla went on her merry way setting out the items needed for the Thanksgiving project. While they were cutting, gluing, and pasting Antoinette thought about how nonchalantly Darla reacted to her mother going on a date, but then again she was only nine years old, and maybe the idea of love and romance hadn't yet entered her mind.

Chapter 21

Lucinda flung her apartment door open almost knocking down the picture on the wall behind it. She shut the door with the same force. Lucinda was angrier with herself more so than anyone else. She knew it was childish and un-Christian to feel the way she did. But, she didn't care. Of course she wanted her friend to be happy, *but why does she have to be happy with the man I like?*

Lucinda kicked her feet out of her shoes, and threw her purse on the sofa. She knew Marcus was all wrong for her, and was just right for Casandra. Anyway; what would she do with a good man like that? She was salt, and he was oil. She was flamboyant, and full of drama. He was very conservative, and full of patience. Lucinda paced circles around the sofa. She had pent up anger, and no one to direct it to—except to herself!

"This is stupid! Why am I tormenting myself, she blurted out? This is something that can never be. I love my friend, and I feel that Marcus may be

really liking her too. But, who is there to love me?"
She tried to hold back the tears. In her moment of
questioning, a quiet, still, small voice came into her
hearing. *I love you Lucinda,* and she knew it was the
Lord.

———

The Server handed dessert menus to Marcus
and Casandra, then cleared the table. Casandra
knew she didn't want to order a dessert. She had
some sweets at home, plus she knew her family
had something planned to celebrate her birthday
on Monday. Marcus had been so gracious in taking
her out she hated to turn him down when he asked
what she wanted for dessert. She found a polite
way to decline saying she was sure she was
expected at her family's house for dessert this
evening, and another small celebration the
following day. She jovially said she didn't want to
encourage her sweet-tooth any more than was
necessary.

Marcus said he understood, but if she could
indulge him, maybe they could share a piece of
chocolate fudge cake together since he wouldn't be
at neither of her other celebrations. Casandra

nodded her consent, and Marcus ordered the dessert, and excused himself while he whispered something in the Server's ear. He said he told the Server to bring them two forks, and reminded Casandra that a sweet-tooth was one of his weaknesses too. Casandra thought, *sure, but it doesn't show up on you like it does on me.* She had to refrain herself from ogling his muscular physique, and his sensuous–though unintended vibes.

Casandra was so engulfed in conversation with Marcus she wasn't aware that several other Servers moseyed over near their table. Once their Server returned (much to her surprise) there was a burning candle on the large slice of cake. The other Servers immediately swooped together to sing '*Happy Birthday*'. Marcus joined the singing ensemble enjoying the surprised look on Casandra's face. After the short refrain he slid back into his seat, and pushed the cake toward Casandra. He said, "Close your eyes and make a wish." As soon as she closed her eyes he reached into his inside jacket pocket and took out a slender rectangle box. He quickly placed it on the table. Casandra really didn't have anything in mind to wish for, so she just asked God for joy and happiness. She opened her eyes, and they fell on the box lying beside the piece of cake.

She was so surprised she just stared with her mouth opened. "Happy Birthday Casandra Russell." Casandra looked at Marcus in awe. "Hey, he said, don't you think you'd better blow out that candle before the wax melts down into the frosting?" She was in such a daze she couldn't seem to move. Marcus reached across the table pulling the saucer toward him. "Here, he said, you better let me do that for you." He softly blew the flame out. Casandra tried to put a complete sentence together, but it came out in stammered patches. "How did you—I mean, when did you?"

Marcus flashed that adoring smile of his again. "Calm down Sister Casandra. I know what you are going to ask me. You want to know how I was able to buy you a birthday gift when I just found out this morning it was your birthday…well, I guess tomorrow is really your birthday. It's easy to explain." Marcus leaned back in his seat, and Casandra thought she saw a shifty look come over his face. "Well, I knew we were going to dinner after service, and I also knew I couldn't leave the pulpit area, so I sent a text explaining the situation to Deacon Campbell, and asked him to drive down to the drug store on the corner to see if he could find something nice for you."

Casandra's eyes enlarged almost to the size of the saucer on the table. Marcus tried to conceal his amusement, but if she had trouble putting her words together before—she was nearly speechless now. "Okay, okay. I was only kidding, he said. I would never do anything like that. I would never expose anything of such a personal nature concerning you to Deacon Campbell, or to anyone else for that matter." He reached across that table and placed his hand on the back of hers. "I'm sorry for upsetting you. I apologize. That wasn't very gentlemanly of me. I feel awful!"

"This is what really happened. Since your daughter said it was your birthday, when I saw you leave out with Lucinda, I figured I had a few minutes to spare, so I dashed over to the church's book store. I wasn't sure what type of gift would be appropriate since we didn't know each other very well. I glanced around at a few thing, and then my eyes fell on this." Casandra didn't want to smile, but one crept on her face anyway. Her smile helped to relieve Marcus' tension. "Whew, he said! I'll never try to tease you with a made-up story like that again. Lady your eyes almost cut me pieces!" Neither one of them could contain their laughter.

Casandra wasn't sure if to open the gift there, or to thank him, and wait until she got home.

Suppose it's something personal? "If you'd rather wait, you don't have to open it now." "No, I can't stand suspense. I'll open it now." *Umm, that's one more little nugget I learned about her today.* Casandra lifted the top from the box. Her eyes lit up in surprise. The two-piece pen set was sleek and fashionable. "Oh, it's beautiful! Thank you." Marcus was relieved and delighted. "I was looking for something useful, but not too personal. I hope its okay. There's not much to choose from in the churches' book store."

Casandra lifted one of the pens out of its slot, and held in in a writing position between her fingers. "This feels really good." Marcus admired the pleasant smile on her face and said, "The note I received from you was so beautifully written; not just the words, but your penmanship too. Your cursive writing is so pretty I figured you were a writer." Casandra placed the pen back in the open slot beside its mate, and thanked him again.

The conversation on the way back to the church was more relaxed—yet still a little guarded. Marcus had a couple of things mulling around in his head he wanted to ask Casandra. He wanted to ask if she would consider seeing him socially on a regular basis, and if he could escort her to the 'Singles' Christmas event. He knew Casandra wasn't a person who dated *any-ol-body* like her friend seemed to, just to say she had a date every weekend—No, Casandra was a little more discreet. If she said yes to either of his proposals he would feel that God had opened the door for the endearing relationship he desired to have with her.

Marcus drove the car to the rear of the church's parking lot and pulled in next to where Casandra's vehicle was parked. He put the gear in *park,* but left the motor running. *Now,* he thought for the *Biggie!* He took in a deep breath, and turned to face Casandra. "Thank you again Sister Russell for allowing me the privilege of taking you out to dinner and for being a part of your birthday celebration. And, if you agree—that is, if you don't mind I would like it very much if we could begin to see each other socially." Casandra was sure her heart was thumping louder than her softly spoken words. "Yes Brother Stillwater, I would like that very much."

Marcus' pulse rate thumped in his ears so much so that he could hardly hear his voice when he asked to escort her to the Christmas event. *But, he must have said it,* because he heard her whisper *yes* again. He opened his door, and went around to the passenger side of the car to assist Casandra as she stepped out of the car. He waited while she fished in her purse for her keys, and when she lifted them from her purse he said, "Here, let me do that for you." He pressed the 'unlock icon' on her key fob, and held the door open while she slid into place. He returned to his car, and waited until she started her engine. He gave her a wave and a warm smile—wondering what it would be like to kiss her goodnight after a date.

Chapter 22

Casandra picked Darla up from her sister's house, and told her she would call her later that evening. She knew she was beginning to like Brother Stillwater very much, but she also had some apprehensions, and those were the things she wanted to seek her sister's advice about.

Darla chattered on about her afternoon with her aunt and uncle. She was excited about the Thanksgiving project, but didn't give her mom too much information about it. She said she wanted some of it to be a surprise. Later that evening when Darla was all tucked in, Casandra called her sister. She told her where they went for dinner, and said Brother Stillwater chose that particular restaurant because he remembered at the church festival she said she liked seafood. That impressed her, but what impressed her even more was the fact that he actually surprised her with a birthday gift. Antoinette was thrilled, and said she kind of figured Brother Stillwater to be that sort of man anyway.

Casandra confessed that she liked Marcus, but after the hurts she went through years ago with Darla's father, she found it hard to trust her heart with another man. "See, she said, I don't even want to acknowledge that he was my husband. I started calling him Darla's father years ago." Antoinette understood her sister's feelings. She felt like she had to handle Casandra's feeling sincerely, but cautiously. "Casandra I love you very much, but when it comes to matters of the heart, you have to trust God to help you. He will show you how to love like your heart has never been broken. You have to turn your heart over to Him so His agape love can cover you. When you love God back in that way, love will flow easily to and from your heart gate.

Everything Antoinette said was true. Casandra made up her mind right then and there not to let the spirit of fear keep her in loneness any longer. She was coming out of the façade of colorful leaves that hid her true feelings. Her season of *Autumn* was over!

Marcus' emotions were all over the place. Now that he was back home he could think of a hundred things he could have done differently, or said better. He consoled himself thinking—well *at least you were brave enough to ask her to the 'Singles' Christmas event, and also if the two of you could become a couple.* Marcus went to the bedroom and got Casandra's hand written note from the nightstand. He read it over again, and the words *'ask me again'* seemed to jump off the page and into his heart. His mind wandered to the Bible and the book of Song of Solomon. He wondered if the way he thought of Casandra was the same way Solomon felt about the *Shulamite* woman.

Marcus reached for the Bible next to the table lamp, and turned to chapter seven in the book of 'Song of Solomon'.

"How beautiful are thy feet with shoes. O prince's daughter! The joints of thy thighs are like jewels, the work of the hands of a cunning workman.

Thy navel *is like* a round goblet, *which* wanteth not liquor: thy belly is like an heap of wheat set about with lilies.

Thy two breasts *are* like two young roes *that are* twins.

Thy neck is as a tower of ivory; thine eyes *like* the fishpools in Heshbon, by the gate of Bathrabbim: thy nose is as the tower of Lebanon which looketh toward Damascus.

Thine head upon thee *is* like Carmel, and the hair of thine head like purple; the king *is* held in the galleries.

How fair and how pleasant art thou, O love, for delights!

This thy stature is like to a palm tree, and thy breasts two clusters *of grapes.*

I said, I will go up to the palm tree, I will take hold of the boughs thereof: now also thy breasts shall be as clusters of the vine, and the smell of thy nose like apples;

And the roof of thy mouth like the best wine for my beloved that goeth *down* sweetly. Causing the lips of those that are asleep to speak.

I *am* my beloved's and his desire is toward me.

Come, my beloved, let us go forth into the field; let us lodge in the villages.

Let us get up early to the vineyards; let us see if the vine flourish, *whether* the tender grape appear, and the pomegranates bud forth: there will I give thee my love.

The mandrakes give a smell, and at our gates are all manner of pleasant *fruits,* new and old, *which* I have laid up for thee, O my beloved."

Marcus slammed the Bible shut. Was it *that* warm in the room, or was it him? *Wow,* he thought, *that's some racy stuff!* He dare not read any farther, because he knew the next chapter was even more involved. He knew from some of his college Bible courses that most scholars agree the Song of Solomon is supposed to be an allegory portraying God's love for Israel and, or Christ's love for His church—even so, one could not deny the overwhelming physical relationship it portrays between a man and a woman. Marcus reached to take his suit jacket off, and realized he didn't have it on. He was more than captivated with the words he just read.

He thought to himself; *O boy Solomon must have been a brother! 'cause he sure knew how to stir his imagination about his woman. I might need to take a few pointers from him.* Marcus knew he needed to calm himself down, but he also wanted to reach out to Casandra just to hear her voice. However there was one major problem—he never got any of her contact information. He sat there smiling to himself. *I bet my boy Solomon wouldn't have forgotten a detail like that!*

Lucinda found herself repenting every time a negative, or evil thought came into her mind about Casandra and Marcus dating. She couldn't help but think things like: *I saw him first. If it wasn't for me she wouldn't have looked that good today. I deserve to know what's happening between them!* "Stop it! Stop it!" Lucinda covered her ears with her hands, and shouted the words out loud. "That's not true, and you know it. Marcus could have been attracted to Casandra even before I was giving him a second thought."

Lucinda couldn't explain her feelings. She didn't want to think jealous thought about her friend, but she couldn't help it. She sat on the edge of her bed, and prayed to stop thinking those negative thoughts.

What's wrong with me? I must be crazy. Do I need

to get some counseling? She pined her way back to the living room and clicked on the remote to the TV. *Maybe I can watch something to get my mind off of my feelings.* She wanted to call her friend, but decided not to, just in case the shadows hanging over her feelings came through her conversation. "Yes, she said, a football game. That'll get my mind off of the feeling of unrequited love." She fixed a few snacks, and sat something to drink on the coffee table in front of the television.

The sports anchor was carrying on about a fabulous intercepted play that had just gone down. It did stir Lucinda's interest, but still, there was nobody to share it with—even if she didn't know what an intercepted play was.

Chapter 23

Lucinda was not surprised when her cell phone rang. Her parents usually called on Sunday evenings to check on her, and she almost said Hi mom without looking at the *caller-ID*. It wasn't her mom, or her dad. It was Casandra. Lucinda's voice almost sneaked up on an ambiguous, "Hel-lo", and Casandra asked if she had caught her at a busy time. "Never too busy for my *Bestie,* she said, and she really meant it from the heart; although even to her it sounded a bit strained.

Casandra thanked Lucinda for being such a good friend. She told her how much she appreciated her birthday make-over, and the jumpstart to a wonderful birthday week. Lucinda let Casandra share her experiences at her own pace mainly because she didn't want to ask any probing questions. Casandra told her where Marcus took her for dinner. Lucinda knew that was one of Casandra's favorite places to eat, but wondered how Marcus would have known that. When Casandra told her about the surprise birthday gift Lucinda exploded with glee. "Stop it girl! Are you kidding me?" Casandra had to smile at her friend's over enthusiastic comments. She and Lucinda were different in so many ways she wondered how they ever became such good friends. *Maybe it's true,* she thought, *opposites do attract.* Before she hung up, Casandra invited Lucinda to the birthday gathering at her sister's house for Monday evening. She said she would be there with bells on at 7 o'clock sharp.

Lucinda sat for a moment still holding the phone in her hand. She could tell Casandra was pleased with the outcome of her date with Marcus—yet she didn't sound wildly excited about it. Lucinda knew that was San's personality. She tried not to let her thoughts go *there,* but they did. *Why couldn't that have been me?*

During their talk Casandra told her Marcus said when they shared the booth at the festival, on their lunch break in the Fellowship Hall he remembered her saying that she liked sea food, and that one of her favorite places to go was the place he took her for dinner. Lucinda leaned back releasing a long yearning sigh thinking about how Marcus remembered that special something about Casandra. She couldn't help but wonder what the men she had dated remembered about her.

Casandra opened the oblong box that held the pen set. She rubbed her fingers back and forth over the chrome plated pens. In the confines of her bedroom she began to reflect on the events of the day. She was not a conceited person, but felt very special that Brother Stillwater was interested in her. There were many ladies at church who she thought were much prettier than her, and surely they were much thinner—*Stop it!* She told herself. *Don't you dare let the Devil steal your joy!*

Her mind turned back to Marcus. She knew of the one children's story book he had written, but during the course of their conversation she found out that he had written two other children's books. He said he didn't depend on book sales to support his living income. He also worked at an advertising agency as an illustrator. Casandra couldn't really think of any area where she was gifted, or had talent in—except for singing. She loved music, but she wasn't about to share that with him on their first date for fear he would ask her again about joining the Praise team.

On the way back from Antoinette's Darla asked her how she liked her birthday date with Mr. Marcus. Darla was excited as any nine year old would be about her mom going on a date, or than again Casandra had to realize that all single-parent children might not be as excited as Darla was. She was also surprised that Darla used the word *date* so casually, because she purposely didn't allow herself to use that word for the mere fact that it could have turned out to be a one-time event—except Marcus asked to see her again socially and to escort her to the 'Singles' Christmas party. But, she didn't share that with her daughter. She let it remain at what had already occurred.

———

Marcus was disappointed that he didn't get Casandra's phone number, but when he thought about it he wasn't too let down. Although he had opened the door to begin a relationship with her, he didn't want to smoother her, or scare her off. If it wasn't for the joy of his first date with Casandra on Sunday, his Monday would have just been routine. Now, he was smiling, and his heart leaped every time the vision of Casandra sitting across the table from him went through his mind. He thought about her enjoying her birthday party at her sister's house.

He smiled thinking about her expressions of surprise each time she would open a gift. Marcus did not realize how much he was smiling until a co-worker mentioned it to him saying; "What's up Bro? Either you just won the lottery, or you're in love, and since you came in to work today I take it you didn't strike it rich!" Marcus had to agree with his friend. He didn't win the lottery—which was something he didn't believe in playing, but he was in love. *As a matter of fact,* he thought, *that makes me feel very rich!*

Chapter 24

By the end of November Casandra had saved Marcus' number in her phone, and they talked a few times a week. They kept their conversations light, sharing things about their jobs, their experiences growing up, and traditional family outings and celebrations. Before she realized it Casandra found herself in expectancy of his calls. The twosome had moved to a place in their relationship where they no longer used 'Brother', or 'Sister' when they addressed each other on the phone. Hearing Marcus call her by her first name triggered fluttering of butterflies in her emotions. Of course her family and friends called her Casandra all the time, however when Marcus Stillwater said it; it gave her a warm stirring inside.

One evening Marcus decided to call his father, eager to share his news about Casandra. Mr. Stillwater knew his son very well, and this was the first time in years he could say his son had been that excited about a lady. Listening to Marcus he knew Casandra had to be someone very special, because Marcus told him he'd been watching her at church for a long time, but he knew from the first time he saw her she was the woman he wanted to be his wife. His dad didn't often give him advice, or make profound statements about his life, but out of the blue his dad said, "The one you have been waiting for has probably been waiting for you." With that statement Marcus felt the courage to move forward, and he knew everything was going to be alright.

On the first Wednesday in December a little before Bible study, Marcus called the Campbell's. He told them he had officially began a relationship with Sister Casandra. He said although it had only gotten to the place of one official date, and a promise to attend the 'Singles' Christmas event he wanted to go out with her again before that happened. The Campbell's knew to hold whatever he shared with them in confidence, and wished God's blessings on his endeavor.

At the Wednesday night service Marcus waited until Pastor Hastings gave him an approving nod to be excused from his position at the keyboard to attend the his meeting. When he came through the door, Lucinda's eyes went straight to Casandra. Belinda Campbell was in the middle of explaining how the gift exchange was going to proceed, and her eyes did not escape the activity of Lucinda's eyes on the persons of Marcus and Casandra.

Everyone was to place their names in the toy sand bucket that was being passed around. Deacon Campbell made sure everyone used the slips of paper he passed out to everyone, and not their own. After all the names were in the bucket and it was passed back to him, he removed each piece of paper, and gave it another secure fold. He said the gift exchange would take place in two weeks because some Singles had previous travel plans, and would not be there for the social event. He knew that meeting would be an extra one, but it seemed like most of them could attend. If they drew a name of someone who would be out of town, they were to give the gift to that person at the last meeting before the event. If they were going out of town, and the person's name they drew would be at the event, then they were to leave the gift with him or Sister Campbell. The Campbell's set the purchase price for the gift exchange at twenty to twenty-five dollars.

Each person held their breath as they dipped their hand into the little sand pail to pull out a name. Sister Campbell laughed at the expressions on the participants faces as they swished their hand around inside the bucket. "Hey, she announced, you don't have to marry the person's name you picked—you just have to buy them a gift." The room roared with laughter. "Remember, she said, pointing to herself and her husband, our names are in the pot too."

Thomas added to the laughter by blurting out, "Then in that case we'd better all hope we pick a name of someone single!" Many pairs of eyes darted back and forth around the room trying to determine if the face they looked on had drawn their name. Deacon Campbell cleared this throat and jokingly said, "No cheating, and no exchanging of names. We're watching the *'seek and search'* looks that are going on. The purpose of the drawing is so you will be able to step outside the comfort zone of your regular circle of friends."

Lucinda had a fleeting hope of drawing Marcus' name, but then she rebuked herself for the thought. She sat clinching the folded piece of paper in her hand, and turned when she heard a slight gasp escape Casandra's lips. She turned to look at her friend's face. It didn't release much of an expression that anyone would notice; except she was sitting next to Casandra and she heard her breath escape. She noticed her friend's eyes had become wider. "What is it? Whose name did you draw?" Casandra didn't say anything. She just closed her hand tightly around the half folded paper, and put it in her purse. She didn't have to say anything, because Lucinda saw her eyes quickly dart towards Marcus Stillwater, and dart away again.

Murmuring voices arose in the room as each person read the name on their paper, but as far as Lucinda could tell—no one was sharing the name they had drawn. She placed her hands deep in her lap, and unfolded the small piece of paper. A feeling of apprehension came over her. She wanted to peek at the name—yet at the same time she didn't want to know whose name she drew just in case she would be disappointed. Slowly opening the paper she shut one eye, and peeped out of the other. *This is silly,* she thought, *you're a grown woman acting like a grade-school kid.* She straightened her face and looked at the name on the paper. DAEMEON WATSON. Lucinda quickly refolded the paper, and tried not to look in his direction. The beating of her heart began to drum loudly in her ears.

The Campbell's didn't want to hold the meeting past eight o'clock. Their main focus was to give pointers on moving out of one's comfort zone helps to accelerate their growth. The other business was to form a committee of volunteers to decorate the Fellowship Hall for the Christmas event. Their treasure had some funds in it, but the Campbell's wanted to use that money to cater food for the party, and not on extra decorations. The church had some decorations they could use, but hopefully the volunteers would add to what was in the church's storage. The deacon and his wife personally planned to purchase gift cards for each of the Singles for their participation in the Fall Festival.

Lucinda raised her hand. *What the heck?* she thought, *since I'm not going to be here the least I can do is help out with the decorations. I want Casandra to have a beautiful evening.* Belinda was glad to see Lucinda volunteer, and appointed her chairperson for the committee. She had an odd feeling Lucinda needed to refocus her mind on *other* things instead of where her eyes repeatedly dashed. Before the meeting ended Lucinda asked if the others who volunteered to help with decorations would meet her at the oblong table near the back of the room.

She quickly prepared a sign-up sheet with ruled lines indicating where they could write their name and other contact information, and said she would get back in touch with them before the week ended. Five, or six people ambled to the back of the room to sign the sheet, and she was surprised to see that Daemeon Watson was one of them. He inched along in line, and Lucinda tried not to look directly at him. She had noticed him more than once in their meetings. It was hard not to notice how tall and handsome he was. She felt a little self-conscience knowing she has just drawn his name.

When he got up to the table she quickly glanced at him, and then looked down at the paper. He had the most stunning eyes she had ever seen. Lucinda remembered thinking how shameful it was that some of the ladies in the group almost threw themselves at him. They even tried to guess where he was going to sit so they could sit next to him, or across from him. But, *then again*, she thought…*Isn't that the same thing I used to do concerning Marcus.*

Chapter 25

Lucinda reached out to everyone who signed up to volunteer. They all agreed to meet at the church that Saturday at 11:00a. The church would be open to the choir and youth for additional rehearsals for the Christmas program, so her committee wouldn't need special permission for the Saxton to open the church for their meeting. She checked with the Campbell's to see if it was alright to use the Fellowship Hall since that's where the Christmas event would take place. That way the committee could get a good idea of the theme they wanted, and what kind of decorations to bring.

Lucinda wasn't quite sure, but when she called Daemeon it seemed that he was very friendly with her—almost to the point of flirtation, but that could have been her imagination. She made all her calls to the committee short and professional; however when she was thanking Daemeon for his volunteering and was ready to end the call he asked her why she was in such a hurry to hang up.

His question caught her off guard, and at the same time set an inquisitive probe to her mind. Did she misunderstand his question, or was it really a slight flirtation? She ended up saying she was trying to finish up all her calls—even though she knew he was the last one on her list. After hanging up she had to ask herself why she saved his name until last. *Did she do it on purpose?*

———

Casandra kept the folded piece of paper with Marcus' name on it in the nightstand drawer beside her bed. She was grateful she drew his name, but was nervous about it too. He seemed to have the perfect gift to give her for her birthday, and it had been so long since she bought a gift for a man. Of course she brought gifts for her brother-in-law, and those gifts she usually give on behalf of her and Darla. She had not purchased a gift for a man since her divorce, and Marcus certainly had a much different character than her ex.

Sitting at work she mulled over what kind of gift to get for Marcus. Several ideas came to mind. She was just beginning to know a little more about his life outside of the church. She knew he had never been married. He worked for an advertising firm, and he authored at least three children's books. Casandra wasn't sure if he had a hand in illustrating his books, or did someone else do it for him. She thought to *'google'* his books on the internet, but that would most likely show the front and back cover, not giving her the *'illustrated by'* info she wanted to know. She decided to go to the library after work to check it out. Casandra smiled at the obvious pun—*check it out.*

Her curiosity proved to be right. *Soo…he is an artist too.* She went by to pick Darla up from After-Care, and on the way home another thought entered her mind. *Why not order his book online for Darla as one as her Christmas presents?* And to add icing on the cake; Darla could have it signed by the original author. That idea took care of one of Darla's gifts, but it didn't solve her dilemma of what to get for Brother Stillwater.

Casandra had another idea, however the limit placed on how much to spend for the secret-Santa gifts might put a damper on what she wanted to buy. *Maybe a trip to the art supply store, or a hobby craft shop will help to pull my thoughts together.*

The meeting opened with one of the Single minister's leading the prayer. Lucinda started right in by thanking everyone for their prompt attendance, and asking for their suggestions on a theme for decorating. All of their ideas were good, but some ideas had to be dismissed because of the group's limited budget. Not wanting to purchase everything entirely new they had to consider the decorations the church already had, and make use of them too. Lucinda also reminded the group that the Campbell's wanted to have ample funds left to host a well catered evening.

They narrowed their final theme choices down to two ideas: 'Winter Wonderland' and 'The Magic of Christmas'. They combined the two suggestions into one theme, 'The Wonder of Christmas'. Their decorations would consist of paper cut-out snowflakes and glitter stars hung from the ceiling. Someone volunteered to bring white pillow batting for the snow, and another person said they would purchase large bags of iridescent snowflakes to sprinkle over the batting. They discussed the area for the caterer, two photo areas; one would be a snowy park scene, also where the band would be, and how many tables they needed for the attendees. The church had a park bench it used for different plays, and some artificial trees. A table would go near the entrance for the Secret-Santa gifts.

The meeting was adjourned with them agreeing to return on Wednesday evening to begin decorating, and they would come back on Saturday for any needed finishing touches. The Campbell's agreed that the Fellowship Hall should be off limits after Saturday. They were going to contact the other *Singles* to let them know their last meeting of the year would be held in the choir room.

Lucinda hung around after everyone left. She wanted to get a good visual of what the transformed Fellowship Hall would look like. She figured as long as the church was still opened for choir rehearsal, and for the play there was no reason to leave right away. She walked around the room a few times pacing out the different spots for each venue.

After a few minutes she decided to sit at one of the tables. She took a pen from her purse, and turned the sign-up sheet over to the other side. Lucinda knew she wasn't much of an artist, but she wanted to sketch out an outline of everything they talked about while it was still fresh in her mind. She was sitting with her back to the doors of the Fellowship Hall, and being in deep concentration she never heard when Daemeon tipped back in.

"Can you use a little more help before Wednesday?" Lucinda jumped when the voice behind her echoed in her quiet surroundings. "Oh, I didn't mean to startle you." Daemeon was as much taken back as she was startled. "I…I just thought. That is I was wondering if you could use another hand in planning everything. Handling something like this can be a tad overwhelming if you know what I mean?" Lucinda just stared at him speechless. She didn't know what to say. She tried to mumble something, but her lips wouldn't move.

Daemeon moved closer and saw the beginning sketches on the paper. "Hey, that's not half bad. That's a good idea to sketch out a diagram." By that time he had grabbed the chair adjacent to hers and sat down at the table. He scooted the chair closer to peer over at the paper "Here, I think I can help with that." Lucinda was glad he moved from behind her; otherwise he would have been leaning over her shoulder to look at the paper. She couldn't believe how his nearness made her feel bizarre. *Why am I feeling like this?* And the very next moment a little voice inside her said—*you can breathe now. And Lucinda, exhale!*

Chapter 26

Darla chattered away about the school's Christmas program, and the part her class had to play in it. All the grades in her Elementary school had a part in the presentation. In music class all grade levels practiced the same songs. The 5th and 6th grades selected three students each to narrate the skits while the other children acted out the scenes.

Darla was selected to read Luke 2:1-16; the birth of Jesus. It was a lot to read, and she told her mother she didn't just want to read it she wanted to recite it. She said the story of the birth of Jesus was one of her favorite stories in the Bible. Reading about the star, the shepherds, and the annunciation of the coming Christ made everything seems so real to her. She said she had read is so many times, she almost knew it by heart anyway. Casandra was a little surprised. She knew that her daughter loved to read, but she never thought she was still reading her Bible book stories too. She brought the colorful book for Darla on her sixth birthday, but didn't realize it was still a part of her weekly readings.

Casandra knew she wasn't what one would call a penny-pinching miser—nevertheless, she liked to be careful of how she spent money; especially around the holidays. She also knew (given her temperament) she could be prone to emotional buying. So, having viewed her immediate cash flow, her savings, and her purposed budget, she found she could be very liberal with her gift buying. She had previously purchased most of the gifts for her family and a few for coworkers, but she never figured on having a gentleman friend to buy gifts for.

Darla's school usually rehearsed for the play during class hours; however on the Thursday night before the performance a dress-rehearsal was scheduled. The parents were asked to either keep their children in After-care, or to bring them back to school at 6:30pm. Darla was already in the After-care program, so Casandra asked Mr. Miller if he would see that she got to the gymnasium on time for the rehearsal. That morning she told Darla what the plan was, because she was going to look for a Christmas present for Brother Stillwater.

Darla was bursting with glee that her mother was a 'secret Santa' to Mr. Marcus. "Mommy, mommy I know what you can get him. It'll be just the present he needs!"

Casandra didn't know how a nine year old girl could possibly know what a good present would be for Marcus—let alone what he needed. But, as not to discourage her enthusiasm she asked anyway. When she heard Darla's answer, she was curious. "A suitcase. Why would you think he needs a suitcase?" "Because, she said. I think the one he carries is kinda old and broken. Sometimes his papers fall out." "Oh, you mean an attaché case." "Yah! That's it, one of those things. Maybe you can buy him one of those." "Wow! That's a good idea honey. I'll keep that in mind when I go to the Mall."

During the course of the day Casandra thought about her daughter's suggestion. First of all she wondered how a nine year could be so observant, and the second thing was why Darla should even care about a thing like that. Casandra knew an attaché case was far most costly than the budget they were given for the 'secret Santa' gift, but it could fit the bill for the personal gift she wanted to give Marcus for Christmas. *Yes,* she thought, *it would make an excellent gift to give him. I'll make sure the gift tag says it's from me and Darla.*

———

Lucinda checked with the Campbell's to see if the team could come to the church before seven o'clock. She said they wanted to look over the decorations that were in storage to see what would best fit their selected theme. Deacon Campbell said the church was usually open around six o'clock for the groups that held their meetings before Bible study. He suggested she notify the team to be there around that time so she would have some of the men to help move the park bench from the storage shed, and bring in the round tables she needed. He also told her not to worry if they needed extra time to finish decorating that he and Sister Belinda would stay after Bible study to lock up the Fellowship Hall, and the church.

The volunteers brought in beautiful decorations. The Fellowship Hall was overflowing with Christmas. That was one of the things Lucinda liked about the 'Singles' group. Everyone seemed to care about each other's well-being, and (as far as she knew) there didn't appear to be any visible jealousy, or envy going on among them—

well…maybe just a little on her part. Nonetheless all was going along fine.

Daemeon had sketched out Lucinda's suggested diagram and ran off copies to tape on the wall so all the committee could see where each station was to be set up. Everything was going along fantastically. The Fellowship Hall was being completely transformed into– '*The Wonder of Christmas*' theme.

After all the venues were set up the team cleared the tables and floor of decorations that weren't going to be used. The last thing to do was to put coverings and center pieces on the tables. They only needed to use about three round tables for the number of those who would be attending the event. Sheila was to set up the utensil table adjacent to where the caterer's tables would be, but it was past time for her to pick up her son from the children's Bible study. She asked if someone could do that assignment for her.

Lucinda was chairperson over the group and had no problem taking on the task. When she spoke up to say she would do it, another person behind her chimed in at the same time to do the task. It was Dameon. Lucinda thanked the rest of the group for doing such a fantastic job, and said they all could be dismissed. A few of them lingered around a little longer to take pictures of the scenes. They were taking selfies in the park scene, and in the decorated photo booth because they were going to be out of town. She even heard a couple of them say they wished they were going to be there so they could enjoy the Christmas party too.

Chapter 27

Casandra was a little skeptical about inviting Marcus to Darla's school's Christmas program, but she was glad she did. He accepted without reservation, and said he would get there on time. Casandra wanted it to be a surprise for Darla. She knew she would be overjoyed and filled with delight.

Christmas was just two weeks away, and the Mall and other stores were filled with shoppers. Casandra's taste didn't lean toward Mall shopping, but the immediate circumstances called for her to go. As a rule of thumb she was a leisurely shopper—although she went with a made up mind of what she was going to purchase she didn't want the hustle and bustle of the crowds to break into her concentration. Not sure of where the music store located, and wanting to save time she stopped at the posted marquee to view the layout of stores in the Mall's. *Humm, maybe I can find my secret Santa's gift in the music store too. That way I can kill two birds with one stone.*

The ring of her cell phone broke into her musing. A quick glance let her know it was Lucinda. Casandra pushed the green talk button and said, "Hey, long time no hear from", changing the familiar phrase of 'long time no see'. "Whatcha been doing?" "Sorry, I've been busy. Being over the decorating committee for the 'Singles' Christmas event has been a bit more challenging than I expected. It also included coming up with a theme, figuring out where to place the venues, and assigning people to different task; plus it all had to be finished in a week and a half."

"Wow girlfriend, you have been busy!" "Yeah, but to tell the truth I enjoyed it. Besides, everyone on the team was so cooperative. You guys are going to love what we've done. Hey where are you? I hear a lot of background noise."

Casandra said she was at the Mall hoping to find her secret Santa's gift. She would have liked to talk longer, but her time was running short. She wasn't sure how long it would take to find the store, or the gift–maybe even two gifts once she started looking around. She would still have to get Darla from rehearsal, pick up some fast-food, and get back home. The evening was already passing quickly because at the first of November they had to set clocks forward an hour. The lady's said goodbye promising to catch up with each other before the holiday began.

———

Lucinda sensed this probably wasn't a good time to share her happenings on last night with her friend anyway. *Maybe it's for the best,* she thought, *since I'm not sure what happened–that is if anything happened. I'd better think this situation through a bit more before I go sharing it around*—although she knew she would only be sharing it with Casandra.

She warmed up some left-overs and sat at the small dinette table adjacent to the kitchen. Her mind drifted back to Wednesday evening. The volunteers had gone, and she took the diagrams off the walls, and Daemeon began setting up the small table that would hold the plates and utensils.

From there they moved their attention to the table coverings and center pieces for the three tables. In just making casual conversation Lucinda mentioned how she thought he had a good eye for decorating. What she didn't expect was what he said next. "Thank you Sister Brown. I usually have a good eye for beautiful things." The unusual remark stunned her, because he stopped what he was doing to look directly in her face when he said it. Lucinda was momentarily thrown off her guard by the stare coming from those warm brown eyes laden with thick black lashes. *Was it the ambiance of the Christmas lighting in the room, or were his eyes saying something more than what her natural ears were hearing?*

"Hey, are you two about finished in here?" Deacon Campbell's voice pierced through the silence of their non-spoken thoughts. "Yes sir, Daemeon retorted, just putting the finishing touches on these last two dining tables." The Campbell's stepped inside the doors to admire the room. "What an amazing transformation, Belinda said with excitement. This doesn't look like Restoration of Hope's Fellowship Hall at all. It looks like—well, it looks like one of those Event Centers across town. It looks like we chose the right team to do this amazing decorating." "Well, we owe it all to this lovely lady right here,

Daemeon said. She is very creative, and she gave inspiration to the whole decorating team."

The deacon and his wife said their goodbyes, but not before Belinda noticed the embarrassed look on Lucinda's face. They told them all the other doors to the church were locked, and reminded the couple to turn out the main light switch in the room, and to exit through its back door. Deacon Campbell cautioned them to be sure they collected all their belongings because the alarms had been set, and the heavy security door would automatically lock behind them.

Daemeon asked Lucinda if everything was alright because she hardly said a word since just before the Campbell's came in. It was true, and now she felt a little stupid that he noticed it. However, she made a polite excuse about being somewhat tired, and relieved now that her obligation was just about over. Placing the last center piece, and grabbing up her things Lucinda headed toward the back of the room. She was about to unplug the lights when she noticed Daemeon had not reached for his coat.

"Now, I know you're not going to walk away from all this beautiful scenery, and not take a picture!"

He wanted to take a couple of 'selfies' of them together in the photo booth, and another of them in the snowy park scene sitting on the bench. Lucinda sat her bundle down, and moved reluctantly towards the venues. They waved and said "Christmas" in the photo booth. She purposely put a little distance between them when she sat in the park scene on the bench. Not knowing that it was done intentionally Daemeon scooted in close to her, and put his arm across her shoulder to take the picture. He looked at his phone demanding a '*do over*'. "This will never do. I know you may be a little tired, but loosen up. Smile. Act like you're happy. After all this is a Christmas photo, not a *Mug*-shot!" The comment made her laugh, and right in the middle of it–the camera flashed.

Lucinda grabbed her hat and coat. They unplugged the Christmas lights, and switched off the main lighting. The Fellowship Hall turned dark. Daemeon opened the door, and when they were on the outside the metal door clicked behind them. The night had become cold, and a light snow had started to fall. Lucinda thanked Daemeon again for all his help, and started towards her car, then stopped in her tracks. "My purse, my purse, her voice echoed in the still night air. Oh no!"

Daemeon turned to see what was wrong. "What is it? What's the matter?" "My purse. I left it inside! I sat it down when we took the photos, and I forgot to pick it up on my way out. I picked up my other things, but I left my purse. I don't have my keys!"

Lucinda was starting to panic. "Okay, okay. Let's try to figure something out. Calm down, and try not to panic, he said. If it will help any I can give you a ride home." "Thanks, but it still won't help because I don't have any keys to get into my apartment. All my keys are on the same keyring." Daemeon took a few steps towards the building to try the church door. The handle wouldn't budge. He didn't want to try again for fear of setting off the alarm. "Well let's not stand out in the cold. The snow seems to be coming down heavier now. Tell you what; I'll start my car, and we can sit in there while I call Deacon Campbell. I'll let him know what happened." He told Lucinda not to worry that everything was going to be alright. She followed behind him as he jogged across the parking lot to open the front passenger door of his car.

He started the engine and said they would have heat in a minute. He called Deacon Campbell and explained the situation. Fortunately, Deacon Campbell told him they had just reached their house, and as soon as Sister Campbell got inside he would turn around and head back their way. Daemeon thanked him, and relayed their conversation to Lucinda. She gave a reassuring smile; although somewhat weak. After all, he had made several suggestive statements that evening. He might have been sincere, but she was on her P's and Q's just in case he tried anything *fresh*. She felt so venerable, and tried not to think about the moment when their eyes locked. She didn't want it to play over and over in her mind…but it did.

To past the time they looked at the pictures Daemeon took of them. He said, "here let me text them to you." "But you don't know my number." "Sure I do, he said. Remember you called everyone on the decorating committee? I saved your number in my contacts." Lucinda had forgotten all about that. In their conversation Daemeon wanted to know who was going to take down the decorations after the event was over. Since most of the team that decorated would be out of town. The plan was for the church custodial staff to take down the decorations, and put them in storage when they cleaned the church for Sunday.

The headlights from Deacon Campbell's truck casted beams of brightness across the car windshield as his vehicle turned onto the lot. He unlocked the security door of the Fellowship Hall, stepped inside and appeared a few seconds later waving his hand toward them indicating that the alarm was off. Daemeon pulled the car closer to the building and told Lucinda he would wait until she got her things. He put the car in park, and went around to open the car door for her. He extended his hand to assist her out of the car. She took notice that his hand gripped strongly around hers. She didn't know if that was normal, or not. After all she hadn't gone out with many real gentlemen who helped ladies out of their cars.

She apologized to Deacon Campbell who was holding the door ajar for her. He told her it was no trouble at all. The Deacon reset the alarm, and closed the door tightly. Daemeon followed behind Lucinda as she briskly walked the few extra feet to get into her vehicle. He stood by the car as she started the engine. "I hope this isn't our last conversation Miss Brown." There was an edge of hopefulness in his voice. "I would like it very much if you allowed me to call you during the holiday." "Oh, I guess that will be alright if you want to", she said in a matter-of-fact manner. "Then I will call you before I leave. Good night"

Lucinda closed her window, and Dameon's car lights followed her off the church's parking lot. For some odd reason she felt safe and warm inside.

Lucy Heath

Chapter 28

Casandra got to Haskell Elementary school early. She wanted to surprise Darla by bringing one of her favorite dresses to wear to do her speech. She also brought along a new pair of opaque tights that complemented her dress. Casandra didn't let her daughter wear tights often, but being as this was a special occasion, and Darla went through so much effort to memorize her entire reading, the surprise would make her feel a little more special.

Casandra parked her car, and went directly to the aftercare room. There were other children there anxiously—she supposed waiting for their parent's arrival, because when she opened the door every face turned in her direction.

Mr. Williams sparked up when she came through the door. Casandra wasn't sure, but there seemed to be a glint of attraction towards her in his eyes. He came over to greet her. "Good evening Ms. Russell. You look very flattering tonight." He usually had a sort of reserved nature about him, but here lately he was becoming more outspoken with his compliments. Realizing his boldness he quickly turned his attention to the other students behind him. Turning back to her he said he had already seen that Darla got to the gymnasium. Casandra thanked him for his compliment, and also for seeing to Darla. Then trying not to acknowledge the pleasurable beam on his face she left through the opened door.

Darla was filled with glee at her mother's surprise. Casandra went to the girl's restroom with her daughter while she was getting dressed. Darla was excited about wearing the opaque tights, and her church shoes with the small platform heel. Casandra pulled Darla's hair back into a pony tail, and secured it with a bright Christmas scrunchie. She gave her daughter a big hug and a kiss on the forehead saying she would be sitting near the front where she could see her, but she didn't spoil the surprise that Brother Stillwater would be sitting there too.

Lucinda was puzzled over her mixed emotions concerning Daemeon. On the one hand she knew how superficial she was when it came to men. She always seemed to be drawn to the first fair-*skinned* handsome guy she met that had hazel eyes, and a beautiful smile. On the other hand, most of them turned out to be *'players'* even the ones in church. But, she couldn't put all the blame on them. *After all, she practically threw herself at them, chasing them down like a hungry dog after a meaty bone.*

Now here she was with Daemeon Watson, who seemed to ignore the ladies flirty ways in their meetings–coming on to her in a very flirtatious way. *Of course,* she thought, *he could just be the romantic type of guy and not a 'player' at all. But, how can I tell the difference?*

Dameon's advances were flattering, and Lucinda believed them to be genuine, but she was used to being in control of her romantic escapades, and now she was concerned that being swayed by Brother Daemeon would leave her defenseless.

Lucinda would have normally called Casandra, but she wasn't sure if this was the night for Darla's Christmas program or not. *Nah, it couldn't be tonight, otherwise she would have invited me.* Lucinda tried to dismiss the thought, but something in the back of her mind kept wondering if she had been jilted for *Mr. Marcus Stillwater!* The picture of the two of them together stirred up ill fillings within her. "Stop it. Stop it, she shouted aloud. 'San San' is my best friend, and I won't listen to you…you green-eyed monster. Get away from me *Now*"!

Lucinda knew she allowed the voice of the enemy to rule over her again, and this time she was going to fight back. Anxiety had begun to creep in. She had to calm herself down. She fixed a cup of chamomile tea. While sitting at the table sipping her tea another thought jumped in her head. *Call her. Ring her phone. See if she answers.*

As if the voice was a real person standing in front of her she raised her arm in the air, and extended her right hand (palm outward). "Be gone you Devil. I come against you in the name of Jesus"!

After that she sat down and let out a deep breath. She smiled to herself, then continued to sip her tea. She sat there with the confidence of a victor having slayed the dragon. The jingling ringtone of her phone broke into her meditating. She reached for her phone, and her calm spirit elevated up a notch, because it was Daemeon.

Casandra stood at the entrance of the school gymnasium doors. She scanned the audience, and spotted Marcus sitting two rows from the front. He was sitting the second seat in leaving the outside seat for her. It was surprising to her how she could recognize his physique, and shapely hair cut from where she stood. She moved cautiously forward, and took the vacant seat next to him. During the play Daemeon looked over at Casandra several times, and smiled. She could feel his eyes on her every now and then, but she only responded a couple of times with a smile. Her smile gave him a warm feeling inside. It almost insured him of a deeper connection.

At the end of the performance all the grades gathered on stage to sing 'We wish you a Merry Christmas'. Some of the younger kids beamed with pride showing smiles with gaps and spaces from missing teeth. One child, she supposed to be a first or second grader, began crying so loudly that his parent had to come and remove him from the group. After the song they all shouted "Merry Christmas everybody!" The students took their curtseys, and the audience gave thunderous applauds; each parent committed to clap the loudest for their own child. Children sprang from the stage dismounting in all directions looking for their parents, grandparents, and family members.

Darla ran straight to Brother Stillwater.

Casandra was happy she kept his coming a surprise; otherwise if Darla knew ahead of time she might have gotten a case of *'the nerves'*, and might not have performed as well. Casandra had to admit to herself, although not a completely negative feeling, she was a bit taken back when Darla ran to Marcus first instead of her, but she had already her just an hour before. Casandra and Marcus kept what few outings they shared very private, and this was the first time—outside of church, or being at the library that they were seen together in public.

Darla turned to her mother and said, (leave it to children to blurt out the unexpected) "Mommy, are you and Mr. Marcus dating?" Casandra felt faint. *Why did her child have to be so loud?* Her mind went blank. She was absolutely stunned! Seeing the look of shock on her face Marcus jumped to the rescue. "Well young lady your mother and I have become very close friends, and as a close friend who admires her, and her darling daughter (he gave the top of Darla's head a couple of light pats) she invited me to your school play. And, I must say you were phenomenal." Darla began to beam over, and Casandra shot Marcus a look of appreciation. He returned it with a gentlemanly nod.

Lucinda's hand trembled as she reached for the phone. She drew in a dep breath, and tapped the *on* icon. There was a space of silence while she was wondering what to say, and then a questioning voice came on the line. "Hello. Hello is anybody there?" Trying to kept her voice steady she said, "Oh, yes. Yes somebody's here…I mean yes I'm here. Hello." As educated as she was, at that moment she felt like a first class idiot.

"I'm sorry. Did I catch you at a bad time? I can call back later." "No. No it's not a bad time. I'm not busy. I was just sitting here…" She let her voice trail off without completing her sentence. After all what was she supposed to say, *I was just sitting here thinking of you.* "Look I'll be flying out tonight, and although we have each other's number, I was wondering if it was alright with you if I attach your picture to yours? I know I want to call you over the holiday, and given the chance you should feel led to call me back I want your lovely picture to pop up instead of 'Wireless Caller'.

Lucinda was dumbfounded. She didn't know what to say. Another moment of dead air fell between them, and Daemeon took advantage of the lull. "I was just thinking we could use the *selfies* we took when we finished decorating. What-cha think?" Lucinda didn't know how he came up with this *we* business. Her voice sounded distant in her own ears, but she heard herself saying, "Sure. That'll be alright." She realized she was only giving two to three word replies, and not really having a conversation. *Think, think,* she told herself.

"I'll be leaving out in the morning, she said." Daemeon wanted to know where she was going. She told him she was flying to Tulsa, Oklahoma. "Oh, my aunt lives not far from there near Oklahoma City. I think it's less than an hour and a half drive away." *Please don't let him say he's going there for Christmas?* Lucinda felt bad thinking what she did, but had the courage to say, "So is that where you're going for Christmas?" "No. I'm visiting my sister, and her two kids in Ohio." "Oh boy Ohio, she said, maybe we'll both have a white Christmas." "By the way he said, Deacon Campbell gave me a secret-Santa gift. He said you drew my name. I guess you really wanted to keep it a secret, because there was no name on the tag. Not even yours. I'll try my best to wait 'till Christmas morning to open it." Lucinda could hear the humor in his voice. They said their goodbyes, and once more this warmish feeling came over her.

Chapter 29

The Campbell's called to thank Lucinda again for heading up the decorating committee in such an excellent way. Belinda also asked if she and Brother Daemeon got alone okay. Lucinda told her they worked together well, and said he was a big help. She left it at that, but had a sneaky feeling Sister Campbell was fishing for more of a personal report. She hoped she wasn't playing match-maker.

Antoinette drove over to Casandra's a little ahead of time to pick up Darla. She wanted to help her sister get ready for the 'Singles' Christmas event. Casandra was grateful because; not only was she a nervous wreck, it seemed like everything she tried to do went askew. Her hands shook when she tried to put on her makeup, and eyebrow pencil, and no matter how she tried her French-twist kept tilting sideways. Before Antoinette arrived Darla helped to zip up the back of her dress, and fastened the little hook at the top of the neck. Her own nails were too long to do it. Darla was happy that her mother was going to the party with Mr. Marcus, and couldn't understand why she was so nervous about it—after all, they saw each other every Sunday at church. To her it was kind of silly to be nervous.

Antoinette rang her sister's phone to let her know she was on her way up. Casandra said she was in the bedroom, and that Darla would let her in.

"Hey kiddo, Antoinette said, are you all packed? Do you have everything you need for tonight, and church on Sunday?" "Yes Mama. Momma's in her bedroom." Antoinette raised a questioning eyebrow at Darla who just shrugged her shoulders, and began to giggle. She teasingly gave her nice a waggle of her index finger, and moved quickly towards her sister's room. Giving the door a few light taps she said, "It's me San, I'm coming in."

Casandra's worried nervousness gave in to a feeling of relief when her sister entered the room. Although there was nothing dramatically wrong she had been feeling overwhelmed. Antoinette knew her sister pretty good, and she was convinced that she was allowing negative voices to engulf her mind again. Casandra looked ravishing. Her clothes, her makeup, and her choice of jewelry was impeccable. The only thing that needed attention was a few more hair pins to straighten and sturdy her French-twist.

The sisters held hands and said a short prayer before leaving the room. Darla had her overnight suitcase sitting by the door, and was anxious to go, but not before she *oohed* at how beautiful her mother looked. Antoinette snapped a few pictures of Casandra standing by herself, and a couple more of her with Darla together. She whispered something special between sisters in Casandra's ear; gave her a big hug, a kiss on the cheek, and headed down the steps with Darla who (all the way down the steps) kept waving goodbye and saying , "Good night Mommy. Have a good time."

Marcus—trying to pre-judge traffic along with the ensuing weather, arrived a few minutes early at Casandra's apartment. When he originally asked to escort her to the Christmas event Casandra agreed, but nervously suggested they drive their own vehicles. That was the one thing Marcus didn't agree with. He said a date meant that the man came to a lady's house to pick her up. He said he agreed with private meeting the other times they began to see each other socially, but this time things were different. It was time to come out of hiding. This was a real bonafided date-*date*, and it was time church people saw them together.

Marcus understood Casandra's apprehensiveness. He told her she had to get over the feeling of not wanting to be noticed. He brought to her attention the Bible verse 1Corthians 13:4-8. He said that particular scripture gave many definitions of what love is—and *convenient* was not one of them. Casandra agreed with him verbally, but in her mind thought, *did he just say he loved me?*

After leaving their coats in the Choir rehearsal room, and receiving a hat-check ticket they entered through the double doors of the Fellowship Hall. It looked like a Banquet Event Hall. It was so beautifully decorated. Casandra wanted to call Lucinda right away, but reframed from doing it. They were directed to the area to their left where a table was draped with a green table cloth to leave their Secret-Santa gifts.

Even though Pastor Hastings was there, the

Campbell's were the official greeters, and welcomed the two of them with open arms. Marcus asked if there was any particular table they were assigned to sit at, and they said no that it was open seating. This time Marcus led the way, and Casandra followed close behind him. He was tempted to grab for her hand, but changed his mind. He didn't want to put any more pressure on his date than she probably was experiencing already.

Casandra kept a plastered smile on her face viewing other groups of *Singles* sitting at various tables. She wasn't able to tell if any of them were paired up as couples, but was very aware of the gawking eyes, and turning heads that followed them as she and Marcus walked past each table.

Marcus spotted the table near the back of the room across from the Caterer's station. He recognized a young lady from the 'Singles' group, and a Deacon and his wife—the two of them must have been chaperones. He asked if the other vacant seats at the table were already spoken for, and the deacon's wife said they were all open except for the two that were saved for the Campbell's. Since the tables accommodated eight people Marcus turned to ask Casandra if the table was agreeable with her.

Casandra nodded a *yes* feeling somewhat relieved. They greeted everyone at the table, and Marcus pulled a chair out for her to be seated. She gracefully lowered herself downward toward the seat keeping her body slightly raised while putting pressure on one foot waiting until he slide the chair in closer, and then she sat fully on the seat not having to scoot in to the table.

The hired band was playing cheerful holiday music. Marcus smiled to himself remembering in times past when he would have been playing for such an occasion as this. But, now tonight he thought (secretly poking out his chest) *I'm here with a beautiful, elegant lady, and she's my date!*

Deacon Campbell came forward quieting the room. He shared two main things; how the secret Santa gift exchange would proceed, and the order tables would be called to the buffet. The rest of the evening all were at liberty to socialize, take pictures at the photo booth, the park scene, and of course; dance to the live band—as long as their moves were decent and in order. All laughed behind his last remark. They gave a hardy round of applauses for the decorating committee, the Caterers, the band, and Hip-Hip-Hoorays for the Campbell's.

Chapter 30

Before the Christmas event ended the light snow flurries had turned into a steady stream. Marcus asked Casandra to wait at the inside doors while he ran to get the car. Casandra could sense the prodding eyes piercing her back, and braced herself for curious questions. Clearing her throat a female member of the Praise team said, "You look stunning tonight *Miss'* Russell, and that dress is so becoming on you."

Casandra picked up on the snooty way she put emphasis on *'Miss'* Russell, but only replied with a thoughtful thank you. "Have you and Brother Stillwater been dating long?" *Humm, do I detect a note of jealously?* Casandra tried not to act upset about it. After all; what could she do about people's feelings? So in a (not so snooty manner) she indicated they had become acquainted at the Fall Festival, and in the previous 'Singles' meeting when they saw that neither of them were going out of town, they decided to attend the event together.

———

The hour wasn't that late, and had it not been for the snow Marcus would have suggested for them to stop at one of those pancake restaurants for coffee. A considerable amount of snow had fallen, and even though it had trailed off he couldn't be certain that it wouldn't pick back up again later on. He verbalized his thought to Casandra, and she agreed.

She said the secret Santa gift exchange was more of a secret shock gift exchange for them when they found they had drawn each other's name. Marcus said he was pleased when he drew her name, but he had no idea she had drawn his. They laughed about it on the ride back to her apartment, but admitted how embarrassing it was, because since they came together everyone thought they had rigged the drawing.

Marcus pulled up in front of Casandra's apartment. He went around to open her door. The fallen snow stood much higher on the curbs and sidewalks than it was on the streets. "No, no, he said. Don't get out yet. Let me clear a path for you. I wouldn't want you to ruin those pretty shoes."

Casandra waited a minute or two while he swept the snow from side to side with his shoe. Marcus portrayed a gentleman's chivalry at its best. She smiled; raising an eyebrow thinking, *he noticed my shoes*. Marcus reached for her hand. "Be careful now." "Marcus, you didn't have to do that. What about your shoes?" "Oh, he said, they'll be all right!"

He kept shuffling the snow back and forth with his foot until he got to the landing of her apartment steps. Marcus, I feel just terrible about this." "I don't, he said. I'm just glad it's not puddles of water!" They both laughed, and Casandra cut her laughter short saying, "I can't let you end the evening shivering, and going home with soaking wet shoes. Please won't you come up for a cup of hot coffee, or maybe you'd like tea." Her sentence almost carried over to say...*or something else*, but she was glad she cut the phrase off. It could have come out sounding unseemly.

Casandra flipped the switch on the entry wall inside the kitchen, and pointed to the living room. "Have a seat." Marcus sat in an arm chair instead of on the sofa, and removed his shoes. Casandra felt a sense of relief although she didn't know why. She collected his shoes, turned on the oven, and sat his damp shoes on a sheet of newspaper on the open door. She said it would just take a few minutes for the coffee to drip, and asked him how he wanted it prepared.

Marcus sat back comfortably in the chair admiring the nicely put together room. The holiday decorations were serene and calming. The room had tabletop scenes of Christmas villages covered with snow. The white twinkle lights under cotton bating looked like a peaceful Christmas card photo, and the iridescent sprinkles of artificial bits of snowflake gave the ambiance of fresh fallen snow on the cozy little towns. It was almost as if he hadn't left the park scene that was set up at the church.

Casandra called from the kitchen asking if he was okay where he was, or if he wanted to come to sit at the kitchen table to have his coffee. He said if it was alright with her he would rather stay where he was. He was enjoying her beautiful decorations. Casandra unfolded a TV stand and sat it beside his chair. She returned with a small serving tray that held his cup of coffee, and a saucer of Christmas sugar cookies. Marcus smiled when he saw the cookies, and Casandra said, (while taking her seat on the sofa) "I remembered your sweet tooth, and we didn't have much dessert at the party."

Marcus thanked her and took a bite of a bell shaped cookie. "Umm, delicious! Do I taste a hint of almond flavoring?" "Yes. I always add a little almond extract to my Christmas cookie dough. It gives the cookies that boost of holiday flavor." Taking a sip of his coffee, and reaching for another cookie Marcus said, "I knew you baked these cookies. They melt in your mouth. You can always tell homemade cookies form store brought." Marcus complimented Casandra on her decorations, and asked if she was a collector of houses for her village scenes. She said she didn't start out to be one, but found she was adding a few new pieces each year.

If it was to be a complete town it needed a bank building, and then it needed a church. One thing led to another: a post office, a school building, the big decorated tree in the middle of the town square, and so on. Marcus sat back and enjoyed her feminine movements and the coziness of her voice as she worked her way from piece to piece explaining how it came to be in that particular town's collection. She had three different town scenes. Actually, one was a busy city. She said that was Darla's favorite. She liked setting up the hotel, the restaurant, stop signs, and traffic lights.

Before he knew it the time had passed into a

later hour than he intended to stay. Marcus voiced that thought, and wiggled his toes. Casandra went to get his shoes, and walked back to the kitchen with his coffee cup and empty saucer void of cookies. Marcus stood and entered the kitchen. Casandra was looking out of the kitchen window. The snow was still falling, and had begun to accumulate. Coming to stand behind her Marcus peeped over her shoulder. Trying not to be distracted by what was harboring in his mind he said, "Wow! I'd better get moving before I'll need a pair of skies to get home." He sled his arms into his overcoat, and said how much he enjoyed the evening–*all of it*. That yearning to hold Casandra in his arms and kiss her emerged again forcefully–although he had managed to subdue it for most of the evening.

Standing at the door Casandra detected a slight hesitancy in Marcus' decision to be on his way; even though he said the hour was late. She wondered had the moment come for their first official real kiss, which she thought about all evening, but felt it was up to the man to make the first move in that direction. A thought came into her mind. "Marcus, if you're not going to be visiting your family for Christmas, I would love for you to celebrate with mine. Darla and I are going to be over to my sister, and brother-in-law's house, and I'm sure they'll be happy to share the holiday with you."

She lowered her eyes speaking softly, and added…"and so would I." Marcus was so swooned by her beautiful fluttering lashes he could hardly speak when he accepted. "Thank you very much, I'll be there." Though not an intentionally rehearsed move he felt his body being drawn towards hers. He put his hand under her chin lifting her face to his. His lips rested upon soft rims of giving flesh that sent explosive beams to all the right places of his being. In almost a hushed voice, he whispered his good night.

Descending the stairs the best he could hope for was that his foot rested on each rung, because at that time he couldn't feel the weight of his own body.

Marcus stood on the front stoop of Casandra's apartment for a few seconds letting the cool chill of snowflakes dust against his face, and then he thanked God that he didn't linger in his kiss…for all the *wrong* reasons. He was thankful he didn't lean his body directly against Casandra's during their kiss, because she was too much of a lady, and he was too much of a gentleman to control what was whelming up in his body.

However, he was still a man made of flesh and blood, and he couldn't promise himself what would happen the next time when he took Casandra fully in his arms.

Chapter 31

Casandra's heart was beating faster than her head seemed to be spinning. She stood with her back plastered against the door, and dare not move for fear of falling. How could her emotions be that distorted? She was full of joy–and yet she could feel the tears streaming down her cheeks.

She slowly wobbled towards the bedroom, and sat on the edge of the bed. The pounding of her heart slowed to where she was able to hear things around her. *Is this what being in love feels like?* Trying to concentrate she removed her shoes and earrings. *I know I really must be in love with Marcus because thinking that I'll never see him again makes me ache in places I never knew I had.* Anxiety was all over her, but she knew it was a different kind of anxiousness, because instead of wanting to run to the kitchen for sweets, and sugar cookies; she felt in desperate need of a glass of cold water.

On the flight to Ohio Dameon's mind wandered back to the night the team was decorating for the Christmas event. He knew it was an awful way to feel, but he was glad Lucinda left her purse in the church. If that hadn't happened he might not have had the chance to sit with her in his car. He remembered thinking…*man, what luck!* He wished he had drawn her name for the secret Santa gift exchange, but he drew Deacon Campbell's instead.

The Singles who were going out of town for Christmas either brought their gifts to the last meeting–if they drew a name of someone who was also leaving, or left the gift with the Campbell's to put on the gift table if they drew a name of a person who was going to be at the event.

He had taken a late evening flight, but still wasn't able to sleep on the plane because of the short trip before the layover to Ohio. Dameon hated having his sister drive to the airport in the late evening to pick him up, but by the time he decided he was going to visit her for Christmas all of the good flight schedules were already booked, so he had to choose from what was left. Dameon smiled to himself thinking that he wouldn't have booked a flight at all if he knew he was going to have a chance to talk with Lucinda.

He'd noticed her a few times in the meetings, and even gave her a gentlemen's nod a couple of times, but he thought she must already have a boyfriend, because it seemed like she didn't respond favorably to him. His second thought was, *what good would that have done for me to stay home. I only talked to her twice, and she was going to Tulsa for the holiday?* Dameon pushed his seat back to relax. He took out his phone, and tapped in his passcode. The screen lit up with the photo of him and Lucinda. He saved the photo booth picture for his screen saver, and the park bench scene for her calls, but he didn't let her know that. A warm feeling rushed through his senses. He wasn't going to phone, or text Lucinda he just wanted to see her face on his pone.

———

Lucinda arranged for her neighbor to drive her to the airport, and to pick up when she returned. Sitting at her departing gate her eyes floated to the posting on the marquee at the gate next to hers: **Oklahoma City.** She must have seen that posting every time she flew back and forth to Tulsa, but this time it made her think of Dameon. Lucinda's eyes floated back to the marquee every so often. It was then she realized a sort of melancholy feeling was coming over her knowing that Dameon was flying in the opposite direction– away from where she was going.

Chapter 32

Antoinette called Casandra early Christmas morning to say she would probably leave church early, and Darla would have to sit with her. She hurriedly asked how her evening went, but by the time she got one sentence out Antoinette went on with her next thought. She could tell her sister was quite busy, and this was not the time to share her evening, nor her feeling; however she did manage to say she invited Brother Stillwater to Christmas dinner. "Oh wonderful, she said, all it takes is setting out an extra plate. Darla brought her presents over last night, and they are under the tree. She helped me with the sweet potato pies, the potato salad, and we made some more sugar cookies."

Casandra smiled at the sound of the inhale of breath her sister took before continuing to talk. It amazed her how much her sister could say in one breath. "Don't' forget to bring the cookies you made. Oh, and I need some more wrapping paper, some tape, and some confectionary sugar if you have any. Oh, she said as she was hanging up, tell Brother Stillwater dinner is at 3 o'clock, but he's welcome to come earlier if he wants because we're waiting 'till after service to open our presents."

Christmas service was scheduled to begin an hour earlier than usual because the Sunday school and youth would be presenting a short skit, and saying their Christmas poem recitations. Casandra knew that Marcus and the other musicians would be a part of the presentation because they practiced with the Sunday school a couple of times last week, so he probably would be coming to church early. She pulled her car in an empty spot near the back of the church. She was nervous for two reasons; first, because of Brother Stillwater's rousing kiss on Friday night, and secondly because of anticipated gossip of the two of them attending the 'Singles' Christmas event together.

A car pulling up beside hers caused her to indiscreetly look out of her window. It was Marcus! *What in the world,* she thought *I imagined he would have been here much earlier than this.* He grabbed some gifts bags out of the front passenger seat of his car, and closed the door with his foot. Casandra didn't move. "Hey, you in there. You gonna sit there all day, or do you plan on coming to service?" Marcus smiled that wonderful smile of his, and an excited calm (if there is such a thing) took over her fear. He nodded towards his arm laden with gift bags, and speaking through the closed window said, "Miss Russell a fellow could use some help here."

Casandra got out of her car and took two of the bags from his hand. "By the way, he said, Merry Christmas. I thought about you all night, and if my arms were empty they'd be holding you right now." Casandra knew it was the middle of winter. She could see their breath escape and linger in the air, but as far as she was concerned it was the middle of spring, and her façaded autumn heart had changed its season!

Marcus was explaining that the packages were gifts of appreciation for members of the band. He said although their participation was mainly voluntarily, and at times they received some sort of gratuity when they went with the pastor to outside church services; he wanted to be a blessing in their lives too.

Casandra hoped she heard most of what he was saying about the band, because her mind was still trying to process his last words about her, and the feelings filtering through her heart. *I've really only known this man for about three months, and I know I'm falling in love with him?* A gush of cool air swooped across her face, and her body shivered. Marcus noticed the slight shudder, and supposing they had stood in the cold too long suggested they go inside right away, however Casandra knew it was something much more profound than the weather. *She was in love with this man!*

She walked with him to the choir rehearsal room and placed her bags in an empty chair. Marcus did likewise, and asked if she wanted to remove her coat and gloves to stay for a few minutes. He knew he had something else in mind that would take a few private moments alone with her—a very special gift. Casandra said she still had a little chill from the cold, and besides that she had to check on Darla. She said it was arranged for him to share Christmas dinner with her and her family, and gave him the address.

Placing her hand on the doorknob, she shyly thanked him again for such a lovely evening at the Christmas party, and said she was looking forward to seeing him that afternoon. Marcus stopped her by placing his hand over hers. When she looked up the unexpected happened. He leaned down and gently brushed her lips with a kiss. Casandra was very much tempted to return to him a kiss of her own, but she knew if she did, it would surely expose what was happening in her heart, and she couldn't let that escape right then and there– especially since they were standing in the house of God on Christmas day.

Chapter 33

The Campbell's were asked if they could leave the winter park scene up until after Christmas. Having peeked in the fellowship Hall on Saturday many parishioners had voiced their desire to take pictures seated in the scenery, and Pastor Hastings agreed. It was so pretty, it would make beautiful Christmas card pictures. So, after morning service many families went to the Fellowship Hall to take advantage of the 'Wonder of Christmas'.

Casandra hurried Darla along to the car so they could get home and change their clothes. Darla wanted to keep her pretty dress on, but Casandra knowing what was best—imagining her opening Christmas presents, and being not so carful at dinner convinced her to change. Besides, she knew that her sister had already taken pictures of her standing near the tree, as well as shots of her standing with the family, and the already wrapped presents.

Casandra searched through her wardrobe for

something casual; yet fashionable enough to wear for the afternoon ahead. It wasn't just that it was Christmas, or that it was Sunday–it was the fact that Marcus would be there, and this would be the first time she would spend time with him with her family. Casandra wondered if it would cause him to be uncomfortable. Nah—if she was honest with herself she was wondering how uncomfortable she would be.

Darla called from the living room for her mother to hurry up. Casandra should have known not to dilly-dally over wardrobe at a time like this. What could she be thinking of? This was Christmas Day, and she was keeping a nine year old on pins and needles! She grabbed a soft mock-necked jersey sweater from the closet, her sued calf-length skirt, and the boots Lucinda bought her for her birthday. Quickly dressing, and taking a look in the mirror she decided to take her necklace off, and replace it with a brightly colored holiday brooch. *That will do it,* she thought. She stuck her slippers in her purse, picked up the cookies and the present for Marcus. She asked Darla to carry the bag of things needed for Antoinette, and off they went.

When Marcus got home he called his uncle's home phone number knowing his dad would have arrived there the night before. His father had a cellphone, but Marcus knew—if they stayed up most of the night walking down memory lane, and went to bed in the wee hours of the morning, it was too early to call his did before he left for church today. Since his aunt and uncle weren't regular church goers he knew his dad probably slept in too. His Aunt answered the telephone, and he wished him a Merry Christmas. Marcus said to let his dad know he had been invited over to Casandra's sister's house for Christmas dinner, and wished them all a Merry Christmas.

Marcus removed the small ring box from his inside coat pocket one more time…yes the ring was still there. Every time he thought about what he was going to ask Casandra today his palms got sweaty, and his hands quivered. He wondered if his timing was right–well maybe not the timing, but the place. *Well I can't help it if I thought I would be alone with her on Christmas at her apartment. How was I to know we would be sharing Christmas with her family?* In thinking about it he had to admit that was a stupid question to ask himself anyway. If his dad wasn't going out of town he would have been spending Christmas with him?

Marcus freshened his cologne and checked his appearance. He had only removed his tie, and changed his shoes. Everything else was okay. He reached for the gift bags that held Darla, and Casandra's present, and headed for the garage. He didn't want to arrive late, but he did have one stop to make. He couldn't go to someone's house for the first time empty handed; especially on Christmas day. He decided to swing by the grocery store and purchase a plant, and a decorative fruit basket. He was sure some were still available.

Mr. Brown sat in the parking spot in the one hour parking lot at Tulsa International airport. Hopefully Lucinda's flight would land on time. He told her to text him when she was at the luggage conveyor belt. That way he could judge when to leave the parking space to swing around and pick her up. He and her mother were excited she was coming home. Somehow having his '*little*' girl home for the holiday made it seem more like Christmas. Of course she wasn't a little girl anymore, and her brother still lived in town, but Daniel lived way over on Admiral and 129th street, and being a working man they only saw him once, or twice a month.

Lucinda arrived at the baggage claim to wait for her luggage. She had only been there a couple of minutes when her phone rang. She knew the plan was for her to call her dad when she was at the baggage claim…so why was he calling her? She retrieved her phone from the outside flap of her purse, and trying to keep her eye on the moving conveyer belt peeked at her phone. It read: CALLER DAEMEON WATSON.

Lucinda let out a small gasp. Her hand shook nervously as she swiped the screen upward. She touched the green phone icon. "Good morning, the voice said. Merry Christmas! Hello, hello. Lucinda are you there?" She was nearly speechless. "Oh, hello." She could barely hear her own voice. "Is everything alright? You sound a little distant." "Yes, everything's alright. I'm at the airport waiting for my luggage." "Oh, then I caught you at the right time." "Excuse me?" "I know there's a time zone difference in where we are, so I wanted to be the first one to wish you a Merry Christmas. Am I?"

Out of the corner of her eye Lucinda saw her two bags roll by on the conveyer. "Oh, no. Darn

it!" "What? You mean I'm not?" "No, no. You are.
It's just that I've been standing here waiting for my
luggage, and when I answered the phone I missed
my bags." "Opps, I'm sorry. When I called I didn't
know you were at the airport." Lucinda spoke up.
"Oh, that's alright. I didn't mean for it to sound
like I was blaming you, and *yes* you are the first one
to wish me Merry Christmas." A slight smile
caressed her face as she moved away from the
crowd to have a more private conversation.

"By the way he said, thank you very much for
my 'Secret Santa' gift. You have good taste."
Lucinda asked if he always opened his gifts this
early on Christmas morning. "No, he said, just
yours. My sister and the kids are having breakfast,
so I grabbed a cup of coffee and came back into
the Den. That's her makeshift guest bedroom." He
said he wanted to open her present last night, but
he forced himself to wait until Christmas morning.
She smiled to herself thinking about the *kid* in him.
Daemeon went on to say he drew Deacon
Campbell's name, and was grateful because it
wasn't hard to shop for another man. He also said
he might have struggled trying to buy a gift for
such a lovely person as herself.

Lucinda was immersed in his words, and had

nearly forgotten about her bags. She said she hoped he was going to enjoy his time with his family, and hoped he was prepared for the cold weather and the snow. Daemeon told her to hang on for a minute he was going to text her a picture of him holding his present. In a few seconds the familiar ding of a text coming through sounded on her phone. She wished him a Merry Christmas, and said she would open the text later, because she was sure her bags had circled around a few more times. She just knew she wanted the text to be a special Christmas present to herself. She hung up the phone, and called her dad to say she was on her way out.

Chapter 34

As usual Antoinette was the perfect hostess. The whole house was holiday ready. Christmas music was playing, and the aroma of turkey and sweet potato pie lingered in the air. Casandra and Darla helped with the last few presents that needed wrapping–mainly for BJ, and for Brother Stillwater.

Marcus parked the car and reached for the gift bags, and other parcels in the back seat. He stood for a moment admiring the outside decorations while trying to balance the fruit basket and potted poinsettia. He could see that a flare for decorating ran in the family. He shifted his parcels to ring the doorbell. From the kitchen Antoinette asked her husband to answer the door. Anthony went to the door with BJ in tow, and made it just in time to assist Marcus with a wobbling fruit basket.

Marcus was glad the ladies were occupied in the kitchen. He headed over to the tree and beckoned for Anthony to follow. He sat the presents down, and lowered his voice. Patting his top pocket he told Anthony he was going to propose to Casandra. Anthony tried not to raise his voice as he shook Marcus' hand to congratulate him. He grabbed a sprig of mistletoe from the tree, and sat it on a side table. The ladies entered the living room with Darla, and the greetings of 'Merry Christmas' was shared by all. Marcus presented the Christmas plant, and the fruit basket to Antoinette, and she thanked him for the thoughtful Christmas gifts.

Marcus was somewhat uneasy about his next move, but he did it anyway. He went to stand next to Casandra, and gave her a kiss on the cheek repeating a Merry Christmas directly to her. Darla let out a slight giggle, but only because she was happy with what she saw. Then Marcus walked over to Darla and said, "and a Merry Christmas to you too young lady", and gave her a kiss on the forehead. She sported a short beam of happiness, and then announced to all she thought it was time to open presents!

There was a lot of *oohing* and *ahhing* and picture taking as each person opened unexpected surprises. During the excitement nobody noticed the eye exchange going on between Marcus and

Anthony who slipped out of the room to get his camera. Antoinette being the hostess she was thought it was time for the dinner to begin, and suggested the remaining gifts could be opened after they finished eating.

Everyone started to stand, and Anthony's eyes locked on Marcus'. He swallowed the lump in his throat, and interrupted the movement. "Excuse me Sister Turner. If I may…I have one gift I would like to present before we eat." Marcus could hear his pulse drumming in his ears. "If we could all take our seats for a moment I won't be long." Anthony gave him a reassuring nod.

Marcus remained standing and cleared his throat. "Casandra I know to you we've only been dating a couple of months, but I've been imagining going out with you for nearly a year. If there's one thing I've noticed about you—and I'm sure those who know you will agree; is that you like jewelry." The room smirked with laughter followed by a few amens. Marcus continued speaking as he walked closer to where Casandra was sitting. "You wear beautiful necklaces and earrings. Your bracelets and watches are very nice too." He eased down next to her on the sofa. "However, there's one piece of jewelry I don't see you wear very often." Antoinette drew in a deep breath when she realized what was about to happen.

Marcus slid from the sofa to rest on one knee. He took the small box from his pocket. Anthony got ready with the camera. "Casandra, I've never seen you wear a ring, so I'm hoping you will do me the honor of wearing this one from me." He opened the lid, and took the ring out of its slot. Anthony snapped the camera. Marcus could feel his emotions rising. "Casandra Russell I love you with all of my heart, and want you to be my wife. Will you marry me?" The camera snapped again.

Casandra's head was reeling. She didn't know what to say. A small voice deep inside her said: "*A time to gather, and a time to embrace. This is your season. This is your* BOAZ.*"* She opened her eyes and said, "Yes! Yes I would be honored to be your wife." Marcus slipped the ring on her finger, and the room erupted with joy. Anthony gave the camera to his wife, and rushed over to the table. He grabbed the mistletoe and hung it over their heads. Marcus took his fiancée in his arms and kissed the woman he had been waiting to declare publically as the one he loved. A camera flashed, but Casandra didn't move. She stayed locked in the embrace of the man God sent to stop the leaves from falling.

Matters of the Heart-Autumn

Lucy Heath

Matters of the Heart-Autumn

About the Author

Heath has the distinctive ability of visually drawing the reader into her character's lives. Using captivating and exciting nuances, there always seems to be a character of intrigue who adds an awe inspiring curiosity to the story line. Although people are committed to their faith, they often battle with right and wrong choices. Heath's novels institute Godly principles without interrupting the captivating flow of a true romantic story. She upholds the responsibility of abstinence for male and female, and by using life experiences, her involvement in drama, twelve years teaching in Christian education, and her studies in biblical theology, this author is able to bring the Word of God through the lives of her picturesque characters as they search their way through questionable daily endeavors, rendezvous and chivalrous acts which draw them to the one they believe God has chosen for them.

Enjoy other Romance Novels by Lucy Heath

Rachel's Forbidden Love

The Reunion: sequel to Rachel's Forbidden Love

Pastor Q and Donna
(A Christmas Surprise)

The Last Time I Saw Love

The Best Christmas Ever

Matters of the Heart, Seasons of Love
(Winter: The Uncertain Heart)

Matters of the Heart-Autumn

www.ingramcontent.com/pod-product-compliance
Lightning Source LLC
Chambersburg PA
CBHW060615030726
47498CB00005B/1684